I0603238

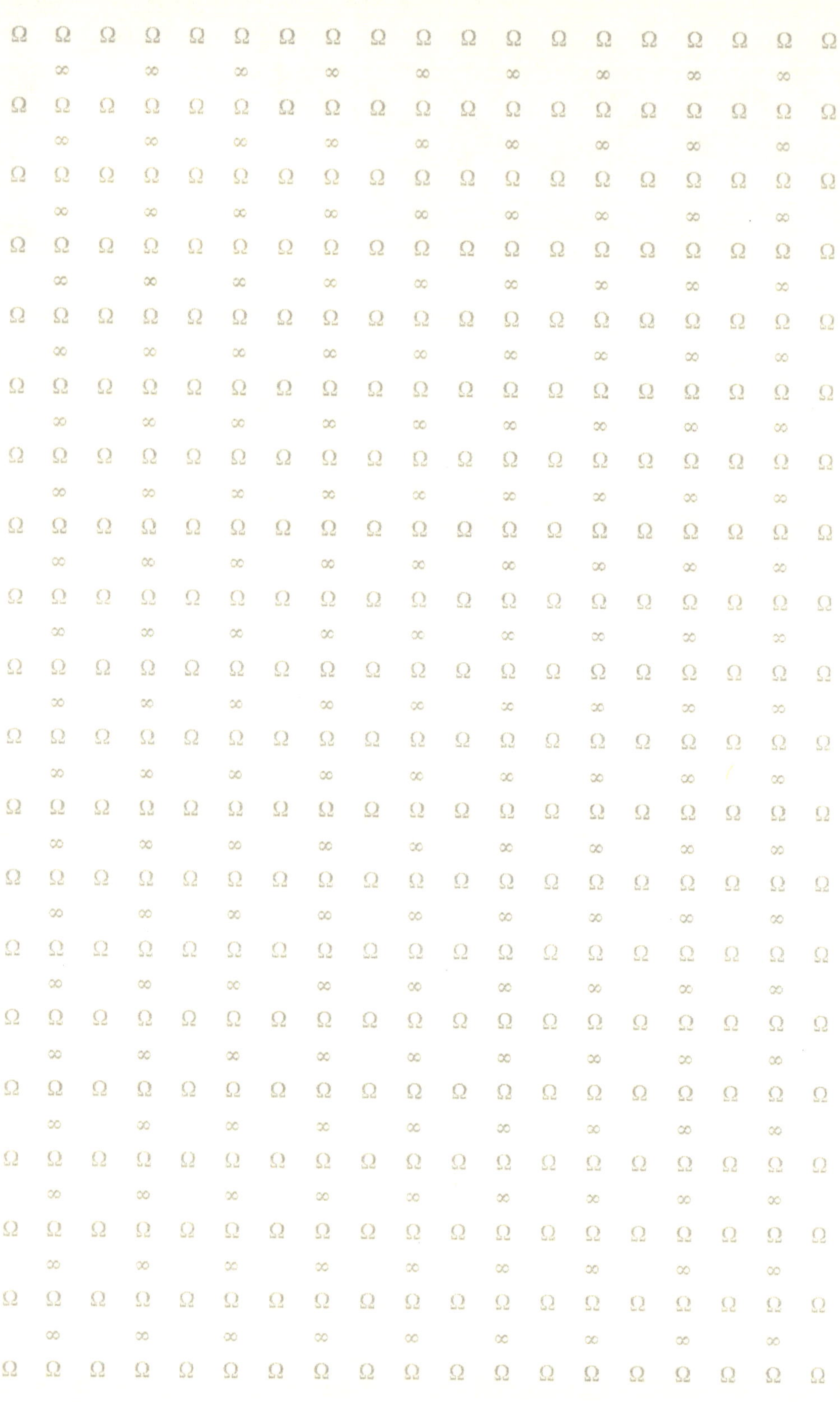

Morrison & Mr Moore

Michael Hyde

Published by **in case of emergency press** 2021

ISBN 978-0-6451280-2-4

Acknowledgements

Where to begin?

My very first writing mentor, Australian writer, John Morrison, for his advice and open encouragement when I began my early hesitant steps as a writer. Also for his short stories referred to in this book. I wish you were still alive so I could give you a signed copy.

My father for writing his wonderful book, '*Betty and Me —a love story*'. Dad's account of looking after my mother for fourteen years when she was beset with Alzheimer's. Most of the Alzheimer's detail I owe to his book and in a way also to my Mum.

My writing friend Robbie Greenberg of *Round the Twist* fame, who on the day he died was still sending me messages of advice and encouragement concerning characters, settings and voice. Who told me this was my best one yet. Robbie got a small guernsey in the story. He also suggested snow domes.

My brother Peter who read every draft and pushed me on. Often telling me what bits he loved. He was in publishing for fifty years and taught me lots.

My partner, Gabrielle for simply being there throughout, responding to every small and large question concerning characters, settings, events and when I started to doubt my story.

My writing students at Victoria University who wrote about their favourite 'spots'. How I loved teaching you and hearing your pieces.

Mallacoota friends Marie and Ian who regularly allowed me free range of their house and veranda while writing. Your company, Ian's and my five o'clock chats while looking at the Lake, watching footy with Marie and our beach walks—all grist for the mill.

Another writing friend Jim Sakkas who suggested, while on a bush walk in Mallacoota, to spend more time on the Alzheimer's aspect of this story.

Our young neighbour Darcy who lives on the other side of the river. Thanks for your comments and for reading nearly every book I've ever written.

The prayer in Cheryl's funeral was taken from *Funeral Resources, Anglican Prayers*. For a non-believer I found the prayer to be not only apt but quite moving.

in case of emergency press

We are proud to acknowledge the Traditional Owners
of country throughout Australia and to recognise their
continuing connection to land, waters, and culture.
We pay our respects to their Elders.
We support recognition, reconciliation, and reparation.

"How often do we tell our own life story? How often do we adjust, embellish, make sly cuts? And the longer life goes on, the fewer are those around to challenge our account, to remind us that our life is not our life, merely the story we have told about our life. Told to others, but—mainly—to ourselves."

Barnes, J. *The Sense of an Ending*

"... if the writer had not had a certain experience he would not have written the story. It's what he does with truth that makes the story."

Morrison, J. *How true is that story?*

Dedication

For all the teachers, lecturers and student writers I've worked with for over 40 years. And those Footscray Tech boys who in the mid-seventies asked me to write stories for them.

Here's one for you.

For my brother Peter who has followed my writing for the same length of time.

You had complete faith in this story from the start.

And again for Gabrielle.

Always there for every book. Always coping with my every up and down, every falter, every fear and every confidence. Love you.

Table of contents

Morrison & Mr Moore

Michael Hyde

SPECIAL PLACE

Buckland's Jetty

I could choose a few different spots. At first I thought of a school camp in Year Seven on the banks of the Buffalo River out past Myrtleford. It was the first camp that I remember actually enjoying which might have had something to do with a few crazies regularly falling into the river. Third time and the teachers took one of the kids into town because they thought he might have hypothermia—his whole body turning ice blue (including his teeth) was probably a good indicator.

It also might have had something to do with a girl who seemed to like being on her own as much as I did. I'd often find her somewhere on the banks of the river or aimlessly following an animal track. When we saw each other we didn't know whether to be pleased or annoyed. Anyway, the camp ended abruptly due to the hypothermia and about six kids being caught having their first choof hiding in the bush.

So, as much as I have fond memories of that spot it's not a place where I have returned to again and again. And there's only one place that fits that bill—Buckland's Jetty. It's not too far from where I live with my grandma. I could go there any time of the day. In summer, in the middle of a scorcher, there's about a billion kids jumping off the jetty into the Bay— bombs, somersaults, attempted swallow dives that usually become belly flops. Lots of noise, screams of laughter, and you can't smell the salt water, feel the breeze or get the stink of sunscreen out of your nostrils. No prizes for guessing I avoid that like the plague.

No, my favourite time for my special spot is at night. Usually after the romantic couples have finished looking dreamily into the water and each other's eyes and the last discarded chip has been eaten by the last one-legged seagull. Any time after 11 PM is good, although I often bump into an old Māori fella doing his bit of fishing but apart from giving each other a nod, we leave each other alone.

Once I start walking on the grey, splintered planks of wood, everything that holds me, everything that binds me, suffocates me, connects me, is gone. It doesn't all slowly dissolve or gradually wash away like the tide. It just goes. Gone. Vanished. Banished. Now you see it. Now you don't.

The sail lines from the boats moored on either side of the jetty clink in chorus from the light breeze, their names revealing their owners' dreams, fantasies, memories and even some Shakespeare: *Island*; *Maggie May*; *Tempest*; *King Lear*; *Rosie*... Some of the yachts have seen better days with their peeling blue paint and hatch doors swinging off broken hinges. You can see faint blurred light through scratched perspex windows where somebody is sleeping, happy to be on their boat even though it only gently rocks at its moorings.

There are of course the rich boats. Spanking paint jobs with the brass and chrome fittings reflecting pale light from the streetlights on the jetty. Their names are far more assertive: *Elizabeth*; *Tiger Shark*; *All the Way*. Titles that show the owners confidence and what school they probably went to.

At the end of the jetty the Māori fisherman dozes with his finger lightly resting on the line, feeling for the slightest of nudges that will make him come alive. I've only seen him catch one fish in all the nights I am here which proves to me that people go fishing not so much for the fish but for the time out, the refuge and the peace it provides. No fisher ever says, "I'm going out to sit by the water because my head and heart needs it." All they have to say is the code, "Gone fishin'"—and everybody thinks they're normal and OK.

I sit down at the end of the jetty, careful not to catch splinters, and look across the bay. A pelican comes into land, manoeuvring its giant wingspan between the boats, like a Jumbo jet, webbed feet stretched out in front for landing, its wings beating rapidly to slow the descent, skidding across the surface as though it's ice.

A few floating seagulls squawk as their sleep is disturbed and some plovers can be heard weeping which bounces off the boats and boathouses, sending a message into the dark waters that spread to St Kilda on the other side of the bay.

I have often looked into this inky blue, past the new grey warship being built (grey's a fitting colour) and the cargo ships piled high with containers lumbering toward port and wondered how far it is to the other side. And whether I could swim it. You know... slip off my shoes, take off my jacket and jeans, slide into the oily water, a small wave to my Māori friend, weave my way through the dinghies and other small craft and off into the wrestling currents which grow stronger as I go. I steal past one of the entertainment boats filled with strippers and vomiting revellers—one of them sees me and yells to his mates to come look at the dickhead in the water, but I swim behind a rickety fishing boat and his mates all reckon he's off his head. Then into the main channel, the jetty lights now indistinct. A darkened, narrow tanker silently appears from behind the breakwater, and I swim for another green-lit buoy and hang on for dear life as the ship and its tugboat pass by, making the buoy and its passenger rise up and down in its crazy wash. Collecting my breath, I strike out again, this time floating on my back where the sky's canopy is torn with cold stars and for some reason I start thinking about my vanished mother, my non-existent father, my solid as a rock grandma and a flurry of other stuff I'd rather not think about. I tread water but discover that I'm travelling at a great rate of knots, past the breakwater, being swept into the shipping lanes, heading towards The Rip and the open ocean...

A ship's horn sounds its melancholy, two, three, four times across the bay and I'm back on the jetty, the Māori fisherman gone and my favourite spot in the world returns to me—Buckland's Jetty.

My jetty.

Morrison.
Year 11B.

CHAPTER ONE

The first time mine and Mr Moore's paths crossed was when I was in Year 8—some years ago now. My home group teacher, who couldn't control a baby, handballed me to the Co-ordinator, Mr Wilson.

I sat outside his office for an hour while he raced around handing out messages, organising late passes and probably teaching as well. When he finally sat me down in his office and did the obligatory, "Well Morrison, what are we going to do with you?" he'd forgotten why I'd been sent to him. He'd left me for all that time. Why? Main reason being that I wasn't causing any trouble. Tell the truth, by Year 8 I'd worked out that they'd leave you alone if you just sat there doing nothing—like watching the school pass you by, checking out chicks, late students, kids having a break from the four walls going to the toilet (or anywhere), whatever, teachers with tablets and papers in their hands (always papers and worry on their faces), Morry the cleaner who had a suspicious scar high up on his forehead. Trick was just keep quiet. Quiet was a big plus for most teachers, and I could keep quiet if I felt like it. Schools reckon they don't mind noise but a lot of teachers I know seem to love quiet, well, the kind of quiet that stops their headaches, the quiet that shows everybody else in the school that they've got good 'control', which in most cases gets a big tick from the higher-ups, other teachers and even the kids who are mongrels but have this crazy respect for the teachers with a classroom full of kids with hormones climbing the bloody walls, being real quiet. Weird, I know. But *not* causing trouble after I had *just caused* trouble always seemed to throw them. I didn't bother telling anybody that I actually liked sitting watching the world pass me by. I didn't tell anybody either that I spent many hours in my own head, chatting away, having a laugh. Most took this as me being the silent type, the 'still waters run deep' type. But I have no idea whether I am what others think I am. I've just been this way since I was a little kid—there'd been plenty in my life that caught my attention, good stuff and plenty of bad. Plenty to keep me quiet and lots to observe. Anyway, why would I tell them about the whys and wherefores—let them get into that and they'd work out some way of really driving me nuts.

The Co-ordinator turned up and beckoned me into his office. His name was Wilson, not a bad bloke but had the behind-his-back nickname of 'little willy'—pathetic eh? No idea if it was small or not and who cares but this is the stuff that kids get up to, to amuse themselves and get under the skin of people who had some power over them. Willy rifled through some papers and without looking at me said, "Well Morrison. Perhaps you could give me your take on why you've been sent to me?" (Translation: 'I've got no idea why you're here—I've completely forgotten, and Ms Rosario should try and sort out these kids herself instead of always dumping them in my lap!")

I kept my face neutral (difficult to pull off but one of the most effective tricks you can use). "Not sure, Sir. Maybe something like late to class."

"Not sure? Not sure? Was it just late to class or something else? Were you rude to her?" Co-ordinators sometimes made a stab in the dark and got it right. I looked away. A kid knocked on his door reminding Willy that he had a class to teach. He stared at the kid, looked down at his desk, shook his head and sighed one of those sighs that come from deep down, from some dark cave that nobody would want to know about.

"Christ. Sorry Matt. Be there in a jiff." Willy turned to me, clearly rattled. I kept my not-happy, not-sad face on. For a second I actually felt for him.

"What was I saying? Oh yeah... were you rude to her? Ms Rosario. Were you?"

"Not that I can remember, Sir." Self-preservation had quickly taken over from any pity I might have felt for Willy. Of course I knew word for word what went down between me and Ms Rosario:

"Morrison! You're late. Again!"

"Wadda ya mean Miss? It's only a few minutes. It's not like it's going to kill anyone."

"I beg your pardon?!"

"Well, what about you Miss. You often don't come on time. And anyway, if something worthwhile happened in my classes maybe I'd make an effort to be on time."

Well, that's the way it went. Smartarse talk, I know. But I was feeling irritated with life in general. Getting into Ms Rosario's face gave me something to do. Amused me I suppose.

The Co-ordinator stared at me, his mind full of I don't know what—his class waiting for him, a hundred other jobs, another grubby little brat waiting outside his office, maybe his wife and kids who he might've had a blue with this morning. The whole thing was annoying the hell out of me. Time for another tack. Time for a small bit of truth.

"Yeah, Sir. Maybe she could've thought I was rude. Not that I was. I was just pointing out she wasn't perfect—not rude but..."

Willy grabbed his folder of work, told me he was sick of having to deal with me, sick and tired of my tangle of words, sick of so many teachers and even some kids complaining about me. And then he did something that surprised me and believe me nothing much surprises me about school: "I don't want you sitting up here like usual, and I want to give Ms Rosario a break. You can go down and sit outside the Principal's office. Don't take any of your books. I want you to go and sit there for a few hours and feel really bored and then maybe you might start to appreciate some of your classes."

"Hang on, Sir. You can't do that. Isn't that illegal?!"

The veins on Willy's face looked like they might rupture. Dark red and then purple. Throbbing like a club light show. Jees, for a second I thought they might burst and cover me with blood and crap. I didn't like where he was sending me, but I didn't want the poor bastard to drop dead either—they'd probably charge me with manslaughter.

So that's how me and Mr Moore first met. 'Met' is probably the wrong word but up until then he knew nothing about me, and I'd only seen him wandering around the school. A pale, oval face, grey wavy hair parted on the left side. Light grey pants, old style polished black shoes and a dark blue tie tucked into his grey V-necked cardigan. The way he strolled around the school reminded me of the way a grandfather might look. Not that I would know. My grandma's husband, which makes him my grandfather, died twenty years ago, about the time I was born, so I only have a stereotyped view of the way grandfathers are supposed to look. He died from being poisoned in an industrial accident in the factory where he'd worked since he was an apprentice boilermaker. I heard this from my grandmother. My mother apparently never took me to see grandma until I was about three and then it was because she wanted a loan. "A loan!? Loaning your mother money was like flushing it down the toilet," was the way my grannie put it.

Anyway, there's Mr Moore in his office with me sitting outside, seeing if I can plug my earphones in without being caught. He keeps his door open and glances at me from time to time. He's been given the run-down on me by Willy so he's not entirely sure about me. I don't know what he expects— he's putting things away in his drawers, possibly things that I might try and steal or use as a weapon. God knows what ideas Willy has put in his head. Watch out for this kid, he's smart. You could find yourself stapled to the back of your door if you give him an inch. Or your favourite coffee mug could vanish and be sold online before you know it. Mr Moore catches me looking at him from outside his door. He keeps on doing what he's doing, slowly closes his desk drawer, then looks at me, his eyes crinkled.

"So your name is Morrison?" The way he said it could've been directed at anyone, but I presumed it was me. I looked at him, pointing a finger at myself, "Me Sir?"

For a second I thought I saw a smile flash across Mr Moore's face but when I checked, it had gone.

"Unless there's another boy out there called Morrison..." Some teachers use sarcasm like a weapon, others couch it in humour. In Mr Moore's case I figured it was the latter.

"Yes, Sir. I'm Morrison." I don't think I'd used 'Sir' so many times in the space of half an hour than I'd used it over the last couple of years. Riverside Secondary College was one of those government schools where most of the teachers allowed you to call them by their first names. 'Progressive' they called it. My grandma preferred 'Christian names' but that's because lately she'd begun attending some Christian spiritualist church. It was one of a long line of churches she'd tried out.

Riverside Secondary College also had a free and easy clothes policy. Another piece of what they liked to call, 'progressive education'. Wear what you like but 'neat and clean', no singlets, skirts not too short and no plunging necklines. I didn't like the last two but as schools go it allowed me to experiment with clothes, dye my hair if I wanted and generally, on certain days, not give a stuff about the way I looked. One guy in Year 10 started wearing petticoats. Not the ones that looked like silky dresses but frilly ones, real frilly. Mmmm—nothing like getting the homophobes up and running.

So once I'd confirmed I was Morrison, Mr Moore went on with some paperwork, asked something of the ladies in the front office, then sat down at his desk and tapped away on his computer. I wasn't sure whether I could look away once we'd settled on my name, so I sat sideways on my chair gazing into his office. Big desk, large window looking out onto part of the school yard, six seats with a coffee table, a half empty bookcase (that surprised me) with one photo on one of the shelves, and a low comfy chair in front of his desk. There were a couple of paintings and framed photographs on the walls, but I didn't have time to check them out properly.

"Well Morrison. You may as well come into my office so you can examine it more closely." (see—sarcasm. Not that I minded—I could be the most sarcastic bastard around and I have to admit, used it more like a weapon.) I stood up and immediately like a well-trained puppy, trotted in. I stood there, not sure where he wanted me to be, standing, sitting, down on one knee, maybe a curtsey. Mr Moore pointed to the chair in front of his desk. When I sat down I sank a few inches, so I had to crane my neck to still see him. I have no idea if he meant it, but the effect made me feel like a prisoner in the dock looking up at the judge.

"So you say your name is Morrison. Is that right, son?"

"Yes sir." (Yes sir, no sir, three bags full, sir.)

A silence entered the room like somebody had just farted. Mr Moore stared at his screen, scrolling around with his mouse. "And you're in Year 8?"

"Yes Sir." (This sir stuff was really starting to give me the irrits.)

"Well... Mr Morrison, you don't seem to appear on any of the rolls, none of the class lists."

"It's not Mr Morrison, Mr Moore. It's just... Morrison."

The old bloke was beginning to show some annoyance. He pushed his computer to the side and looked squarely at me. "OK Morrison. It's Morrison what?"

I moved forward on the sagging chair. I had no idea when I decided to call myself Morrison that it would cause this kind of trouble. "Ah, nothing. Just Morrison."

Mr Moore pushed his chair back, took off his glasses and spoke to me like I might have been a bit 'backward', a bit soft in the head, a bit slow—all those expressions which are supposed to be the nice way of saying a person's retarded.

"Now, son. When your parents enrolled you in this school, what name did they give you?"

"But my parents didn't enrol me. My grandma did."

A sharp edge was creeping into Mr Moore's voice. "OK. Your parents didn't enrol you. What name did your grandma provide when she enrolled you?"

"I'm sorry Mr Moore. She filled it out, so I have no idea what she wrote."

Mr Moore got up from behind his desk and perched himself on the edge. He rubbed at his forehead, grimaced and looked at me over his glasses. I could see he was trying to work out whether I was messing with him or whether I was perhaps, not the sharpest pencil in the box (phrases like this all came from my grannie's extensive collection of sayings). In fact I wasn't messing with him—I was avoiding what came next.

"OK Morrison." Mr Moore was working his tail off to sound neutral, which is a useless thing to try—nobody can sound neutral. "When you were born, what name did your... what name was given to you? I mean, what were you called?"

I stared at him blankly, then looked out his window. Hot flushes rushed over me, pinpricks of sweat spread like measles. I took a quick look at Mr Moore who waited while I tried to get it together.

"It's alright, son. I'm not angry with you. Just need to know your name so I can make sure you're properly enrolled in the school. If you're not then that's easily fixcd, we'll just have to..."

"It's Norman. Norman Healy, sir." Saying the name was enough to make me sick in my guts and a headache like a metal band clamp around my head.

"You OK son?" Mr Moore asked. "Do you need to go to sick bay?" He was concerned enough to put his hand on my shoulder. I couldn't look at him or anywhere. There was that terrible silence again until I said, "All good, sir. I sometimes get these dizzy spells. But all fine now." I smiled wanly and finally Mr Moore went back to his chair and his computer.

"Ah, here you are. Norman Healy. 8B. Ms Rosario." Mr Moore seemed relieved that I now actually had a name, a home group, and a home group teacher. There you go. As long as you have these tags everything in the garden is lovely. Everything schmick. Everybody in their place. Everything in order. Age. Address. Serial number. Date of Birth. Qualifications. Intended profession. Yes Sir. No worries Sir. Present and correct SIR!!

But of course nothing was right. I sat hearing a non-existent clock ticking time away. Waiting for what I knew Mr Moore couldn't help asking. Tick. Tock tock. Finally completing his tasks, the old guy got up and moved to one of the comfy chairs around the coffee table.

"Come and sit over here, son."

'Son' was one of those non-committal terms. Mr Moore had at least realised that calling me Norman wasn't going to be very well received by me—which he could've done if he wanted to be the big man and lord it over me. So on the scoring card in my head I gave him a tick for not being an arsehole. But that didn't mean he was ready to call me Morrison now that he knew that wasn't the name on THE ROLL. Not a bad enough mistake on his part for me to take away the tick I'd given him.

I walked over to the little coffee table and sat down. Mr Moore looked out at some kids mucking around, squealing and giggling, outside his office window. They seemed happy, even joyful. Quite a bit different to the kid sitting opposite him. He smiled at me and fumbled around in his pocket and pulled out some mints. He popped one into his mouth and offered me one. I'm fairly suspicious of any free handout that comes my way, but I took it and hoped that Mr Moore wasn't some secret kind of paedophile where offering lollies was the first step.

I can be a bastard like that. The smallest kindness and I'll pretty soon turn it into its exact opposite. An innocent, 'What's happening?' and if I'm in a dark mood, in my head I'll quickly stretch that to, 'Why do ya want to know? Why would I bother telling you what I've done and what I'm about to do?! Go and stick your nose into somebody else's business' and so on. But I took it anyway. Yeah I know—such a nice boy.

"You know son (there it was again)—when I went to school, lollies in the classroom weren't allowed. If you were caught you'd get the strap." Mr Moore chortled, enjoying his own memories. "The strap," he repeated to himself. "God help us," he almost whispered.

"Anyway," he started like he'd just remembered I was sitting in front of him, "you call yourself Morrison. Does anybody else call you that?" He offered me another mint.

"Nearly everybody, sir." I thought I'd better return to formalities. Mr Moore was moving into friendly zone, something I'd experienced with adults and especially teachers and I didn't trust it all that much.

"So all the teachers and students woke up one morning and decided to say, 'Good morning, Morrison'?" The idea of any of the students saying 'good morning' made me crack up—inside my head of course. I smiled this smile that I invented years ago—not too broad, not too bland, just right.

"Don't think it was quite like that, sir. I think they sort of heard about it and went along with it."

Some of them might also have remembered, on a particularly bad day some months before when I lost it. This kid worked out early on that I wasn't real fond of my name, don't ask me how, some kids have unerring accuracy when it comes to hitting other kid's weak spots. The tiny chink that detonates and shatters what's left. He started to do that sneezing trick where you sneeze and say the annoying word as you do it. It's usually reserved for swearing or whatever in class. In this case he'd sneeze and say my name, the name. He didn't let up. It was lunchtime, around the back of school. I stood in front of him, his name was Chris, and asked—no, not asked, told him to shut his mouth. He didn't. So as I was eating a pie at the time, I decided to share it. I rammed that pastry delicacy into his stupid face. I'd only taken a bite out of it so there was plenty to go around. Plenty of hot meat gravy. Yeah, that stopped the sneezing. Chris squealed like a baby pig, which got the attention of the teacher on yard duty, which got me into Willy's office again.

Don't make the mistake thinking I'm some street wise brawler. I'm not but I knew on some level that on the rare occasion when I got into a fight something snapped where my outside cool fell away and a raging, frothing, livid monster took over. The monster didn't sidle up and slowly possess me. Nothing like that. Zero to one hundred in a second. Before long Chris' sizzled face and my looney behaviour got around the school and around the streets and soon after most kids thought I might be a nut case, so they were happy enough to call me Morrison.

Teachers went along with it too. I was already in enough trouble and the worst smartarse around so they might as well call me Morrison. No sense in adding to their woes. But Mr Moore was different. When he asked a question it seemed like he wanted to know, like he was genuinely interested in the answers. But I'd had so many counsellors and primary and secondary teachers and social workers talk to me I didn't really trust the words, which is strange because I like words— maybe not the spoken ones so much but the written ones. I loved them. One of the rare things I can say I love. Spoken words can be dressed up so you don't know whether you're coming or going. It's those on the page I trust more. Not sure why. Maybe it's because they sit there and you can go back to them and check out their honesty, their bullshit, their take on things, something new, something old...

"Well I suppose I could call you Morrison too, seeing that everybody else goes along with it," Mr Moore smiled. It was an old smile which is the best way to describe it. After years of living, the sun and the wind and the rain, joy and pain falling on it, lines around the eyes and mouth become crevices, as if the face has seen it all, done it all a thousand times so it doesn't have to work hard to show sorrow, happiness, laughter or anger. All the contours are already there, and the face simply falls into line.

"But... Morrison," Mr Moore half smiled, pleased he'd been able to say it, "I'm sorry but I'm intrigued. Where did you get 'Morrison' from? Was it somebody you knew? Or... maybe you just dreamed it up?"

I was already becoming bored with this chat with the Principal. The whole thing had gone on too long for my liking and because I'd been polite and eaten his mints... anyway the bell had gone for lunchtime and I was hungry and realised that Willy had put me there for punishment, so I wanted to get out of there, even though 'out of there' wasn't much better than being there with the old guy.

I fiddled with the lolly wrapper, twisting it into a bow and untwisting it. "I'm not sure, Mr Moore. Probably came to me when I was sitting there one day hating my name." Damn, stuff it. That's the trouble with talking. You go one more step and that's a step too far—now I knew what the next question was. But the old fossil didn't ask it. He didn't say in that oh so neutral tone that's supposed to hide any eagerness or any desire to help: "Well, hating your own name, eh. That's a bit unusual. How long have you felt this way? And why the Morrison bit?"

Instead Mr Moore looked towards the door leading into the front office and said, "I think that was the bell. I'm sure Mr Wilson didn't intend you to miss out on your lunch." He stood up, and as he did so I heard a soft cracking sound and Mr Moore winced. He bent down and rubbed his knee and said apologetically, "Bad knees I'm afraid. Age catches up with all of us. You better get going, son... Morrison. Try and not get into any more trouble, eh?" I smiled and turned to leave. "But it's been good to meet you." He shook my hand. "You don't get to speak to students much when you're a Principal. Especially when you're an old Principal on his way to retirement."

That was my first real meeting with old Mr Moore. It could've been a lot worse. But I was in Year Eight and didn't fully get how strange it had been, how kind he'd actually been. And it went on like that for years. Every now and then Willy or someone who could get away with it would really crack it with me and send me off to sit outside Mr Moore's office. Sometimes he'd chat, other times he seemed too busy. Strange thing was that he never gave me the usual rant of how disruptive I had been or could be. I never told anybody about the chatting side of it. As far as everybody knew, the kids, teachers, secretaries, vice-principals—there was bloody Morrison again parked outside Moore's office. Which suited the powers-that-be very nicely. If I was there, at least they didn't have to worry about me.

However, as I said, that was how it started all those years ago. But it wasn't until Year 11, when everything changed between me and Mr Moore. I don't know if he changed, or I did but things changed. In fact, everything changed in such a short time. Like the blink of an eye. I've been thinking heaps about what happened in that year, and I didn't really know why it was important to get down, but I knew I had to someday. That if I loved writing this was as good a story to start with as any.

CHAPTER TWO

So what is the answer to Mr Moore's question all that time ago that I should've, could've given to him then and there? But it takes a while to know some people and in my case it usually takes years for me to reckon I know someone. Enough to spend a bit of time with and not feel like walking out, getting bored, irritated... .

It's not all that complicated but maybe that's because I've been living with it for ages. To start with I have a father—apparently—some man who donated his sperm to my mother. Not in the IVF sense but in the sense the two of them had a brief relationship, shagged, she got pregnant, had me, then my father pissed off, never to be heard of again. My mother who was already on the skids decided to become an addict which was clearly the best way to raise a kid (get used to my sarcasm because it's not going to stop). Anyway I ended up at my grandma's who did all the raising.

I'd been named Norman Healy, after my father. I keep referring to him as my father but from now on it'll be better if I just drop that. All throughout Primary school I'd heard my name called out on so many rolls and lists, my 'Here' became automatic, which might be the reason why I hate rolls and regimentation so much. But sometimes I'd hear the name and wonder who it was until some kid would dig me in the ribs or a teacher would say something really new and creative like, "Wake up Norman. I presume you're here, seeing you're standing there." I should have replied, "If you can see me, why do I have to remind you?" but my smartarse schtick didn't really emerge until secondary school which won me as many friends as enemies at the time.

Of course if you had a great dad who was called Norman Healy and a loving family with a Mum who made you lunch and kissed you when you came home, instead of a complete absence and a woman who was reputedly your mother and not one who got out of bed and away from the TV only to score, then the name would have filled me with delight, instead of making me feel like crap.

It came to a head late in Year 8. I'd turned thirteen and it had been a hot blustery day with a North wind blowing all through lunchtime. Enough to send an unsettling mood throughout the classrooms and make the kids and teachers all a bit ratty. I was in English, which was my least hated class—even today I have a problem with saying that I loved English. My teacher was Frankie, about as Aussie as they come with a big Italian background. Short, a fabulous pasta belly, usually covered by a Simpson's T-shirt or one with a smart slogan or question on it, 'I know I am, but who are you?'. He was OK as a rule, but I was suspicious of his friendliness, his little chats with some troubled kid after class, his bringing to class some leftovers from the latest Italian celebration— he'd tried to have one of those chats to me in class and when he was on yard duty, but I wouldn't crack. I'd had a lifetime of sympathetic faces and worked out early on that sympathy mainly made those offering it feel better about themselves. I warned you about how nice I could be…

Frankie took the roll, and it was one of those times I had these feelings like there were ten octopuses inside me, fighting over who was going to get control of my guts. Even though I'd taken off my jacket I still felt like a boiled crayfish when my name was called. Frankie said it three times while looking dead at me. A kid in front of me, think his name was Billy, turned around and said in this moronic voice, "Hey Nooooormaaan, wake up ya dickhead." I didn't need much encouragement. I jumped out of my seat, grabbed him by his collar and yanked him onto the floor. Frankie moved quickly for a man with a bit of lard on him. He was at the scene of the crime before you could say, "How dare you!" which he didn't but he came pretty close to saying, "What the…". Instead of throwing me out or sending me to Willy he put his hands on my shoulders and guided me back to my seat, helped Billy up and looking daggers at me saying, "Save that kind of rubbish for people with no brains, if you don't mind Norman." He saw me bristle when he said the name but ignored me and began his lesson on short stories. I don't think I raised my head that whole lesson, staring at the cream plastic-topped table and the attempted artwork of dicks and tits. Strange thing was that I can remember almost everything from that class. Frankie chatted about what makes a short story, gave us the names of some international short story writers, a few Americans, like Raymond Carver then some Australian ones, I can even remember a couple of their names, Lawson, Prichard, Hardy, a few modern ones like Cate Kennedy but had decided he'd read out one that he particularly liked. It was 'Murder on the 1:30' by John Morrison. It was about this young guy who's a writer sitting in a train on its way to Bendigo, while the other passengers talked about some recent murder. My head was still in the story when the class finished and Frankie said to me, "I think you and I better have a talk."

Outside the room with kids yabbering, shoving, tripping, pointing, dawdling, Frankie pulled me aside next to a row of lockers. "Y'know I can't have that kind of stuff going on, mate." Frankie had instinctively gone for 'mate' instead of my name. That at least impressed me. I nodded and looked away. Some of the other kids were checking out the telling-off. There wasn't much to see which shows there doesn't have to be too much different going on at school to capture the attention of bored minds.

"So what was the problem? Did something go on before between you and Billy? Gees mate, you went off your head."

It would have been easy for me to look away, for me to do the shrug-and-I-don't-give-a-damn attitude but I'd been doing that for what seemed like my whole life. I looked hard at the locker until that became stupid so I said straight out—

like straight out, "I'm named after my father and he means nothin' to me, he's never been in my life, if I saw him in the street, which I wouldn't do because I have no idea what he looks like, I wouldn't bother, m'mum was about as useless as tits on a bull too which is probably why she chose him to have me although I reckon they didn't actually think about having me, and every time I hear my name it sounds like it belongs to someone else and every time it's there I wish to hell it wouldn't be."

Now it was Frankie's turn to stare at the lockers. Here's this thirteen year old kid who's just spilled his guts when all Frankie thought he was going to hear was some little kid's petty squabble—instead, he got this whole rant. I could feel tears trying to bust through a dam wall I'd built a long time ago but that wasn't going to happen. One thing to spill your guts, another to stand there blubbering.

Frankie put his books and laptop on the top of the lockers and leant his back against the wall. No wonder, the poor bastard. A few kids were hanging around at the top of the stairs, so Frankie used this to give himself a breather. "Off you go, you guys. Class started 5 minutes ago. Go on! And you, Ahmed, you can stop trying to hide your can of drink." He watched them head off, just slow enough to show they were tough—yeah, real tough.

Frankie drew a deep breath, like he hadn't had fresh air for the last week. "Suppose you've talked about all this to someone?"

"Oh... kind of, not much though." What Frankie didn't realise was that this had been the first time in my life that I'd said so much in such a short space of time. In a way I was as shocked as he was. "OK that's what I figured so it's not much help for me to suggest going to the counsellor and all that bit."

I nodded.

"I s'pose the name's the thing you want to get rid of? You can change your name, you know. You don't have to do it by deed poll or anything, you can just do it."

"What? Just change my name? Choose one out of a hat and from then on everybody calls you that?"

Frankie laughed. "The second bit might take a bit longer. Nearly the end of the year. You could change it over the holidays. But you'd have to check it out with grandma I think."

I smiled. I actually then and there smiled. Not fake either so it felt weird sitting on my face. Yeah, Frankie was OK.

"So do you need a note from me explaining why you're late?" Frankie asked.

"Probably not, sir. I think they're kind of used to that by now."

Frankie shook his head in a phoney 'you are very naughty boy' kind of way. "Off you go and have a think about it. And don't forget you have to read those short stories by next week. The ones by Cate Kennedy and the other by John Morrison."

He gathered his stuff together, gave my shoulder a squeeze and walked off. I mumbled thanks but I don't think he heard me, which is a pity. Not many have heard that come from my mouth.

Chapter Three

This is a hard story to tell and I'm not too sure if other people will get it. I don't mind it being difficult, but I do mind raving on about me and Mr Moore and discovering that the only person it'll mean much to is me. But what other writers say is that when you write a story, if it means bugger all to you then you might as well write it on toilet paper just before you use it.

But maybe none of this story would've happened if it wasn't for Frankie putting me onto John Morrison. That night I went home after finishing my job at the local supermarket collecting trolleys. Best thing about my job is you're on your own most of the time and only sometimes do you have to bother passing time with the other workers and the customers seem pleased enough if you just give a nod or something that passes for a smile. The boss asked me if I wanted to move onto packing shelves or learn the register. "She's right, Andy. Happy enough doing this." Andy grinned. "Sure about that? At least you're not on your own all the time." Andy sidled up to me and nudged me in the ribs. "Get to chat up some of the women going through." Wink wink. I unhooked the cord holding twenty trolleys together and guided them into the bay. "Don't think I could handle all the attention, Andy. One word from me and they'd all want me." My boss hesitated, then thought I might've been joking, "Whoa, we have a Casanova on staff," and wandered off laughing to himself. "Let me know if you change your mind."

My friend, Roxy, who got me the job, worked on the registers—she reckoned all she had to do was to go into automaton mode and tap away and smile and think about photography and films—which was her particular thing. Roxy was my closest friend—probably my only friend—she never tried to get into my head, could be more silent than me, didn't call or text me all the bloody time and for some reason neither of us wanted to have sex with the other. It wasn't a 'friends with benefits' type of thing, although I probably had a few fantasies about her that she never cracked onto. But as much as I liked her, me being a checkout rooster didn't grab me.

The idea of having a good reason to stare at some of the fine looking, long-legged girls was lip-smacking, but having to do the friendly sweet talk to every customer, starting with, "Hi, how are you?" would be enough to make me want to hide in the till. In any case, the opportunity to trot out some smartarse lines and complete fabrications would be too much to resist. "Hi, how you doing?" would get the obligatory, "Fine", "Good thanks" and "Yeah and how are you going?" A reply of a smile or "Pretty good" would be all it took, but would I pass up the chance to deliver something special? "Things could be better. Dad left mum and my three baby brothers and ran off with his secretary to live in Spain. He took our only car and Mum discovered he'd cleaned out the bank account, all our furniture has been repossessed." Scan unsalted butter. "Centrelink's already asking if Mum can take care of all us kids, then my littlest brother, Godfrey, got whooping cough because Mum forgot to get his booster." Scan soy ice cream. Pause to see how the customer's reacting. Slightly enlarged eyes, trying to take in all this tragedy. Checking the line behind her, a weak smile. Time for the zinger. Glancing sideways, dropping my voice, "And as if this wasn't enough for my poor Mum. Hope this won't offend you, but Mum's just discovered that our father gave her a genital disease—like a parting gift." The customer stares at me, like an owl. "Sorry madam. Shouldn't have gone on like that. Don't know what came over me. Would you like me to pack the meat separately?"

There you go. Eventually I'm sure that complaints would start to emerge from the aisles. And the amusement it would provide me means that the stories would become more outlandish as time wore on. Not that I don't have those kinds of story lines doing cartwheels in my brain all the time. My imagination has been my lifesaver as far back as I can remember. Right back to the nights where I lay in bed, listening to the TV droning, maybe music at 50 decibels, cackling laughter and arguments, thousands of them, over anything: "Where's me ciggies? Which one of youse arseholes got 'em? Don' bloody grin at me. Ya slack moll. You and your boyfriend can piss off. Go on, piss off!" The door slams and then one minute later it's, "Hang on you bastards. Where you goin'? Hang on, I'm comin'." And some door in some house in some place would slam and a little kid would lie there, with the covers pulled up to his nose, dreaming up something that would make him feel as though everything was at least average.

Most of those memories are hazy, dipped in mist and fog on good days, slime and grit on others, while some only come out when something changes, or a car backfires, or somebody smokes a brand of cigarettes, or I step off the footpath onto the road. And even then I'm not sure what I'm remembering is real or not. Some of them I put together in my head. Adding bits and pieces, taking out stuff that doesn't fit or doesn't please me until what I have might be a kaleidoscope that seems more real than the actual event. No wonder I was seduced by writing. You start off with a spark, maybe out of your own life and by the time you're finished you've got a story you'd swear was more real than my Granny. This is part of the problem with my story, this story about me and Mr Moore. I think I'm putting it down as it happened but who knows? Maybe it's not so much the details but the heart and soul of what happened those years ago that really matters.

So—I go home and Granny's dog, Einstein, a border collie cross, gets off the couch next to her and makes sure I know I'm welcome and that he loves me, which he does by licking me about a hundred times. I don't like it, especially if I think too much about where his tongue has been, but I let him do it, so his feelings aren't hurt. He was called Einstein because Granny reckoned he was way smarter than most humans she knew. If the humans in my life are anything to go by, I reckon the bar has been set pretty low.

I don't bother interrupting Grandma—she's watching QI which she says helps improve her mind, but my suspicion is that she's got a crush on the presenter, Stephen Fry. As far as I know, he's gay but why destroy her fantasies? And as far as I know Grandma's not gay either. She and Walter, a good old friend of hers go out to the movies every fortnight. Grandma tells me it's just for company, but I've seen the way they look at each other when he comes to pick her up in his ancient Holden and the rest doesn't bear thinking about. I mean, it's fine for old people to be still interested and all that but I prefer not to think about it.

Grandma has my chops and veg under tinfoil in the oven with a slice of Coles apple pie on the kitchen table. I slip into my room and watch fifteen minutes of yet another American murder mystery (CSI in Pasadena, CSI in Tijuana, CSI in Disneyland, CSI in Ballantyne...). I finish eating and start reading. Cate Kennedy is pretty good. Don't mind it at all. But when I start reading, 'Murder on the 1:30' something changes in me. I didn't just change; something actually went off inside me. Like detonations. The short story's all about this would-be writer on a train from the city to Bendigo. He writes in a notebook the whole journey. Meanwhile as passengers get off and on there is a discussion about a murder. The passengers are full of the mystery, all with their own bits and pieces of information, their own theories, their own fears and suspicions thrown into the mix. It's a longish journey but towards the end one of the others turns to the bloke taking notes and asks him what he does for a living. He replies he's a writer to which the other comments that the trip must've been a great thing for a writer to listen to. The would-be writer guy then says something like, "I'm sorry, I was too busy taking notes, working on a murder mystery, you see."

OK the idea in that story is as obvious as dog's balls, probably as obvious as elephant's balls. But here's a writer in the middle of an unbelievable event, a murder in fact, swirling around him and his eyes, ears, heart, brain—everything—is closed. Lights are out. Shop well and truly shut. While there's all this stuff going on right outside the shop door. I got online to find out more about John Morrison. There was an old photo of him. Long face, thinning hair, dark-rimmed glasses, maybe even a bit severe but I see some mirth, a twinkle in his eyes. His bio was there too. Migrated from Britain as a young man, went jackarooing in the outback, became a sailor, wharf labourer, gardener and so on. All that life experience obviously gave him plenty to write about. Morrison also had something to say about anything political. He wrote all his life, mainly in the 1940s, 50s and 60s but never stopped working—a couple of novels but mainly known for his short stories. Most of which he wrote after a hard day's labour. Not an easy time of it which made him and his take on life all the more intriguing to somebody like me.

Next day I wandered into the library at lunchtime, which was not an everyday event for me. Mrs Jacobs, the librarian, beams. "Well, hello Norman, what brings you here? This *is* a pleasant surprise." Now, there's a couple of things going on here. For starters, seeing me as a pleasant surprise is probably the last thing that Mrs Jacobs actually thinks behind her gleaming grin. She threw me out of 'her' library so many times teachers wouldn't even bother including me in those classes. In fact, one time I was caught with an ink stamp I had made at the local newsagents, with the words, 'ex Libras Morrison', which I discovered was Latin for, 'from the library of Morrison'. I had stamped approximately fifty books before I was spotted. Mrs Jacobs simply got up from behind the counter, said in this flat tone, "Come with me Norman," and led me once more to the chair outside Mr Moore's office. A space that was fast becoming known as Norman's Corner. It wasn't a corner at all, but I suppose it had that smell about it being ' the naughty corner.' At least when 'Morrison' became my name it was changed to Morrison's Corner. Be thankful for small mercies, my gran says.

Not only did Mrs Jacobs toss me out, she was also one of the few women teachers who insisted on being called 'Mrs'. She even had it on her plaque in front of her when she was on the desk. Most of the other female teachers were called by their first names or 'Ms so-and-so'. This gave me three options at that time: calling her 'Ms', 'Miss' or calling her 'Jackie'. First names are so easy to find out—overhearing other teachers talking to her, casually reading her mail left on the counter, yelling out 'Jackie' in the yard and see her swivel. I have no idea why some teachers think that calling them by their names is so damn embarrassing or somehow undermining their authority. I can tell you that some of the worst blues I've ever had have been with teachers who I called by their first names. When I was having those eruptions their first name wasn't the only thing I called them.

"Hello, Mrs Jacobs." (I wasn't a complete idiot; I wanted her help.) Mrs Jacobs did the beaming thing again. "Hoping you might have a book I'm looking for."

She narrowed her eyes ever so slightly and ran her eyes over my face. I'd dyed my hair blue at the time, something I did every now and then to get over the monotony of life. She didn't comment probably because she had a streak of red rinse through her hair and any comment she made might just get one back that she'd deserve. Mrs Jacobs' suspicions were on high alert. She probably thought I was going to ask for the latest porn magazine or one of the novels in the library which were well known for their pages about anything even slightly sexual and every sex position you could imagine. You never had to search for the right page—just hold it up and the book would magically fall open to the pages of desire.

"What's the book?" she asked a bit more curtly.

"Frankie got us to read a story by John Morrison. Do you have any more of his?"

"Who?"

"Frankie, my English teacher."

"No, I know who he is." Mrs Jacobs didn't much like other teachers getting kids to call them by their names, much less Frankie who she was highly suspicious of because of his clothes. "I mean the author—John Morrison. Australian author."

The librarian's face went blank, then flushed, then went through a number of other emotions all of which boiled down to the fact that she didn't seem to know who I was talking about. "Well, let's see. I'll check our collection." Mrs Jacobs clacked away but never once said, "I'm afraid I don't know that writer." I didn't come looking for John Morrison to see that confusion and embarrassment on her face—that was a bonus.

A few minutes later she says, " Ah yes. We do have one. It's a collection of his stories. I'll take you down there". Mrs Jacobs escorted me to the last stacks ('escorted' is the right word—keep this kid under tight control otherwise the library's likely to go up in flames). She fossicked around on shelves full of dusty books that didn't seem to have any of the usual letters and numbers library books have. "Here we are," she said, holding the book away from her as she blew off a few centuries' dust. "These are all the books nobody seems to want."

Once more she escorted me back to the desk and didn't ask for my library card. She knew I wouldn't have one. She wrote down my name and the title, handed it to me and smiled that smile that'd turn anybody into a diabetic. As I walked out the door, I couldn't resist it. "By the way, Miss, do you want to read this when I'm done? In case anybody else comes looking for it? I mean, so you'll know next time?" Pathetic? Yeah but it doesn't pay to be so up yourself.

I went home and started reading. Short stories mainly— *To Margaret; Bo Abbott; Flowers; Pastoral*—he wrote about everything. From watching nature as he waited for a bus in the Dandenong Ranges to blokes arguing over a winning lottery ticket, to the romance of a gardener. I read an article, *How true is that?* and another short story, *The Judge and the Shipowner*. That last one got me, nailed me, maybe because it was taking the piss out of the rich and the law but more probably because it was a satire about how much people in authority as well as being loaded, care so much for the poor and downtrodden. As if. Satire is like sarcasm on steroids so obviously I loved it. I read all of them in two days, including at work. I'd perch it on one of the trolleys and read it as I gathered the wayward trolleys. Sometimes I felt like I was a shepherd tending the flock. I was on night shift which meant I could stay at the back of the carpark and read under the streetlight. At one stage Andy came looking for me saying there were no trolleys in the shop. I slipped the book under my jacket and explained that I'd been up the street finding the ones dumped in the gutter. Andy knew I was bullshitting but couldn't figure out what I'd been doing so let it go.

Few days later I was in English. There was some discussion about the short stories, but I didn't put in at all. Most of the kids liked Cate Kennedy compared to good ol' John Morrison's story which they reckoned was old-fashioned while Billy asked why we had to read boring stuff about a train ride where there'd been a murder and we never got to find out who did it. "I mean, Frankie, there wasn't even no blood or nothin'."

There was a reason why I hadn't said what I thought. Usually I don't have to have a reason for not saying much in class but this time I wasn't just being an uncooperative prick, this time it was close to the bone. Frankie, to his credit didn't push me for anything but after class he caught up with me.

"Hey mate," he said putting his hand on my shoulder. "Didn't say much in there. Not that you do most of the time. I'm interested. What'd you think? You read them?"

I looked at his flushed face and nodded.

"And?" he asked.

"Cate thingo was cool. Read her."

"And Morrison? Sorry but I know you got that book of his from the library. Mrs Jacobs told me."

"Did she?"

"Yeah. Funny but she's hardly ever said a word to me. Told me when I was having a coffee at recess."

"What'd she say? That on the way out I stole some stuff, paper clips and pens maybe?"

Frankie chortled. "Nah, nothing really. She looked a bit shocked."

"Did she tell you she didn't know who he was?"

Again Frankie laughed, this time right out loud. "Nup, think she missed that bit of information."

I smiled. Frankie was alright. "Well if you wanna know I reckon he's ace, like really cool. Yeah he's old fashioned and that but he keeps it simple and... and... y'know, like he feeds your brain."

Frankie couldn't stop smiling which was my cue for saying, "Hey Frankie, if you don't mind, don't tell the other kids... and teachers... about this, I mean, what I think and that."

Frankie fiddled with his laptop and folders in his arms, then looked at me quizzically. He shrugged and finally said, "Sure, OK. Don't quite understand but OK."

For once in my life I felt as though I owed someone something. We'd been talking for a while and the bell had well and truly gone for the start of the next class. Frankie walked off but I called him back. "Sorry Frankie, I don't really understand why I don't want you to either. But it's probably because of that name thing you said the other day."

My English teacher had the feeling I was going to tell him something important, not something like the usual kind of crap students dump on their teachers: 'I got no lunch money', 'My parents are arguing all the time', 'My best friend's great-aunt just died, and I think I have to go to sick bay', 'My time-of-the-month hasn't come, can I go outside for a walk?' On and on and on.

"You going to change your name, Norm... sorry mate, it slipped out."

"Yeah. I'm going to do it slowly. Might be better if I do it after we finish with the short stories."

"C'mon mate. The suspense is killing me."

"Morrison."

I immediately felt like the biggest dumbarse in the world. Frankie stared at me then looked away. To this day I thought tears welled in his eyes, but I felt so bloody stupid I couldn't look at him. Frankie continued to say nothing but nodded and kept on nodding. Finally he said, almost in a whisper, "OK, OK. Fine. Good." Then he shook my hand and said, "Let me know when you want me to let others know. Let me know when you want me to start calling you Morrison."

And that was it. Took a couple of months and a few blues here and there, like when I smashed the hot pie into the kid's face and one or two kids and teachers who tried their best to take the piss out of me: "Sooo, Morreeesun, will it be a different one next week? Maybe you might go back to good ol' Nooooorman." My answer was always the same and it shut them up good and proper: I'd start out by stretching or distorting their name, whatever it was, Daaaaaaaveeed, Sooooooozin, Angel for Angelo, "Well if you don't have the right to be called whatever you want, we could all start calling you by whatever name we felt like calling you." Their imagination, if they had any, did the rest of the job. And they certainly didn't want it put to the test.

Grandma didn't mind at all when I told her. She couldn't stand my vanished old man, hated him in fact. And she'd never even met him. Einstein wagged his tail like he was swatting flies, so I had his vote.

Chapter Four

The only other person I told where my new name came from was Roxy. We sat out the back on some rocks looking down at the lazy old river that ran behind the school. Of course that's where the school got its name from—Riverside. It used to be called West Ballantyne but then all the schools started to have this battle to get kids enrolled into their schools, so they came up with fancy names. One school that you wouldn't send a derro to, suddenly changed its name to Lakes Secondary College because close-by was something that looked and smelt like a swamp. So they changed their name and introduced uniforms—all grey of course—which apparently convinces parents that it's a real school with loads of homework and loads of discipline.

"So... you going to tell me where the Morrison bit comes from?" Roxy hid her cigarette from the patrolling yard duty teacher.

"What're you hiding your ciggie for? It's only Matty Simons, y'know. He doesn't bother. Except to ask if he can bott one."

"That's why I'm hiding it. It's my last one," Roxy smiled. She looked up at me from her mysterious green eyes, through her fringe she'd recently died jet black. "Morrison?" She gave this quizzical smile, her dark red lipstick emphasising the question.

"Better than bloody Norman don't you reckon."

"Maybe," Roxy said. "Guess I'll get used to it. Think I better get used to it or you might shove a pie in my face." She flashed a big grin. "But where did you get it from? Get it from one of your Facebook friends?"

"Very funny, Roxy. Leave the sarcasm to me." The Facebook jibe was a running joke between us, mainly because while I had a Facebook account I had almost no 'friends'—mainly because I kept on rejecting requests and didn't ask to be anybody's friend. Except for about half a dozen people, which included Roxy and my grandma. One 'friend' was some weirdo called 'Placebo' from overseas whose interests included Australian platypuses and medicinal marijuana. "Weirder than me," I thought, so I accepted him for a bit of entertainment.

So I told her about Morrison the writer and what Frankie had said and how cool his stories were.

"What's so good about them?" Good question. I examined the outside walls of the school; large cracks meandered their way over the grey rendering.

"Not sure. But he writes about people and places like around here. Y'know—ordinary people. People with nothing, or not much. Ordinary jobs. And he writes about the bush. Trees and stuff."

"The bush!? Since when did you like the bush? You told me the other day that your idea of hell was camping."

I looked down and grinned. "Yeah well, maybe but I do like looking at trees and rivers and stuff."

Roxy shook her head and stubbed out her cig. "Well, c'mon MISTER Morrison, don't want to be late to Media." Media was one of the subjects we often took together. I kind of liked it but Roxy was mad for it, couldn't get enough of it. She thought film making was something she could do for the rest of her life.

As we walked back into school I said, "Hey Rox. Why don't you change your name? Call yourself after some actor. Marilyn… or maybe just Monroe." Roxy gave me a look that looked seriously like death, mutilation at best.

It was in Years Nine and Ten that I started writing stories myself. Nobody saw them except Frankie who saw maybe two and Roxy who read most of them. Nobody else. Not even grandma who probably would've been glad to read them. Once she asked what I was doing on my computer, pounding away late into the night. "Homework, Grandma, just homework. They never let up."

"Never mind, dear. I'm happy you're working so well. Your old Grandma didn't do good at school. School and me didn't mix too well. Goodnight Morrison."

"Mmm," I thought. "Apple doesn't fall too far from the tree."

So that's the way it went in those years—writing stories, hanging with Roxy, working at the supermarket, living with grandma, school—and of course my regular stints outside Mr Moore's office. I'd often see him wandering around the school, the yard, the street outside when school had finished for the day. He'd nod at me, maybe a smile but never talked to me. It was only when some teacher plonked me outside his office that he talked to me. Most teachers didn't even bother sending me to the Co-ordinator who would then put me on the conveyor belt down to Mr Moore's office. They just skipped those stages and got me to where I was going to end up anyway. Nobody bothered with me; I was like a pet dog waiting patiently for his master. But at least when I sat there I could zone out, listen to music if I could get away with it, think about stories I was writing, wonder how I even got to be at this school, wondering why some teachers even bothered to become teachers—like old Ms Cottrell, the English teacher for instance, who decided years ago she should devote her life to working class kids but at the same time didn't understand them or their interests and seemed hell bent on taking the kids to 'a higher plane' of 'culcha' and taking them on excursions to movies which no-one understood and art exhibitions (often by her friends) which nobody went to except Ms Cottrell and her flock. Her favourite novel was *The Prime of Miss Jean Brodie*—an 'extraordinary classic' she called it. She regularly tried to teach it to her Year Nine classes who regularly went on strike and didn't read it. A lot of kids weren't deeply into reading or books as it was, so a novel about Miss Jean Brodie, a teacher who taught her female students about her love life, travels, art history and 'the classics', wasn't exactly going to entice kids into reading. I tried reading it once and fell asleep in the first chapter.

Sitting there I wondered too why some teachers seemed to love their job. Even the weird ones. Jack Kettle was a well-known hypochondriac who taught English, History and anything else the school wanted him to fill in for. Jack's classes might have had different subject titles, but they all rolled into one. The whole school knew his list of ailments—bad back, gout, molars giving him trouble, migraines—the best one happened when I was in a class next door to his. Suddenly the door flew open and in came Jack holding his ample belly and in a stage whisper said to our teacher, "Mate, look after my class will ya?! If I don't go to the toilet now I think I'll fill my pants." After he left, the whole class packed up, including our teacher who sat there shaking his head. But there was one thing all Jack's students agreed on. His classes weren't boring and in the words of Roxy, his subjects weren't specifically about anything—'we just talked about life.'

I used to sit there in my appointed spot, my face in a daydream, checking out the stream, the bunches of kids going to and fro, this class that class, that teacher this teacher, yes miss no miss, need a drink sir, need to go to the toilet, did part of my homework, no the dog didn't eat it, can't do detention tonight I've got basketball, no I don't think I'll play NBA, NBL's rubbish we only get the leftovers, I never said I loved him, that was Julia, what've we got now? Stuffed if I know...

The kids I knew at Riverside you could count on one hand, although quite a few knew me, probably due to my semi-permanent rental outside Mr Moore's office. There was one mate, Johnny Carbone, who left school a year ago. Brilliant footballer, played in the local comp with the Ballantyne Tigers and then snapped up by the Brisbane Lions scouts. We were good friends for a couple of years, but he grabbed hold of the Draft and moved up there. We chat a bit but not much lately. Different lives I guess.

Then there's 'petticoat boy'. We don't talk much but I reckon we got a bond—I changed my name, had a shitful past life, used my tongue like a weapon—and then there's him who's got the balls (presumably) to wear different style petticoats every day. He does Media so that's where we see each other. I have no idea what his name is, but he sails through school life with this smirk, as though he knows exactly what everyone is thinking.

And there's Terry. I caught sight of Terry when he arrived at this school. A few years younger than me. One of those kids. Small, pale, skinny as a sheep in a drought, hair straight like a mop, hides out in the library. Just like a little mouse. One of those kids who other kids his age want nothing to do with. Not that he does stuff or anything that's annoying, except he keeps to himself and gives you the idea that he knows loads about anything and everything. And his major attribute for me is his mouth. I've heard him give it to kids who have a go at him—no obvious put-down except the bully boys know he's had a shot at them but don't quite know what or how. I instinctively keep an eye out for him. He might be able to look after himself, but I doubt it and it doesn't hurt a kid like Terry having someone who has his back.

And of course, Roxanne. My friend Roxy. Others think she's strange, a touch bizarre, not only for her dyed hair and her kaleidoscopic outfits but most likely because she hangs out with me. She even appears to like me. She's stayed over at my place and not once have we come on to each other. Although grandma has her suspicions. Not that I knock back any advances from women—I think I've been checking them out from a very young age. And there's no age restrictions as far as I'm concerned. Only the other day Roxy caught me ogling a thirty year old woman. When she slapped me on the arm I laughed and said, "Rox, the canvas just gets bigger." Then she slapped me again.

So there I sat, like a fungus growing on the wall to the point where no-one knew what I'd actually done. I'd always been there. I didn't even raise an eyebrow. Except for one exception—one of the two vice-Principals, Warren Hamm, who could never resist having a crack at me when he walked past. "You sleep here now do you, MISTER Morrison?" "Tried to set fire to the school?" "What colour hair this week, son?" "Why not a rainbow? You could go in one of those Mardi Gras." He'd walk off down the corridor, cacked himself at such brilliant remarks. I usually shut my mouth around him but so far I'd dreamt up approximately one hundred smartarse jokes all revolving around his name. And his body. You know how people own dogs that look like them? Well Hamm's name had produced lots of parallels to his physical appearance. This time I couldn't resist and as he cackled his way down the hall, I snorted like a baby pig. More of a squeal really. Hamm stopped and barrelled down on me. "What was that Morrison? Or is it still Norman?" The last bit was enough to make me let loose and plant one in his bulging belly. But I kept my powder dry—he'd keep. I looked innocently at him. When he had another go I thought that the odds were stacked against me, so I told him I was singing along to some music I was listening to. Hamm ripped the earphones out of my ears, listened, grunted in derision, and told me he was confiscating them. I'd been listening to 'Wakeup', a Hip Hop band I was into. I liked Hip Hop—bit of poetry mixed with some hostility and a don't-stuff-with-me attitude. The kind of music aimed at dicks like Hamm. Not that he'd ever get it.

Mr Moore emerged from his office to see what was going on. Hamm was red-faced. I actually thought he wanted to punch me. Mr Moore took in the situation, looked enquiringly at the vice-Principal who blustered, "This boy needs some manners, Mr Moore. I'm confiscating these—" He held up my phone and the earphones grasped in his fist, shaking them like a trophy from a battle. Flecks of white spittle foamed at the corners of his mouth which had run out of words. Hamm nodded at Mr Moore and stalked off. Mr Moore watched him go and I swear the faintest of smiles began to colour his old grey face. But he quickly turned and went back inside his office, closing the door gently behind him. I admit I was a bit shaken by Hamm's tirade and was taken aback when Mr Moore opened his door a few minutes later and with a wry smile said, "I think for all our sakes Morrison, you'd better come in here and do your time."

"Just sit over there," he said pointing at the comfy chairs. "I've got some work to do and if I leave you out there you might be murdered, or Mr Hamm might have a heart attack." I mumbled, "Thanks," and Mr Moore went back to his desk. I sat there on the comfy seats like a dormant volcano that had had enough of being inactive. There was hot scarlet lava pouring through me, white-hot rocks and ash that Hamm was slowly, ever so slowly sinking into. By the time it reached his chest he'd stopped screaming and pleading, his eyes staring like a poor dumb animal about to be put down.

"Well Morrison, haven't seen you in a while." My fantasy was interrupted by Mr Moore who sat opposite me, offering me another of his mints. "I thought you'd maybe decided to stop doing whatever it is you do that gets you outside my office."

It was the early days of Year 11, and it was true. I hadn't made it to his office for quite some time. Maybe teachers like Ms Rosario found it easier to just let me be, to just not worry about my punctuality, attendance, homework, my silence. It's rare teachers will take that path because most of them take their jobs seriously. They have this religious fervour about learning. Ms Rosario probably still had this belief, but she could hardly spend so much time on one kid who seemed hell bent on giving her a hard time. I couldn't blame her. Anyway she got pregnant which made me let up on her. It was always weird when you saw your teachers do something normal like having babies—and if you took this to the extreme, how bizarre it was to imagine Rosario and her husband doing it.

"What's going on in your life, son?"

Now this is what I mean about Mr Moore. He could've banged on about school, my subjects, what I was doing next year—but no, he asked a question that I could frame answers to in a hundred different ways. But none immediately came to mind. I think I was still caught up in fury land.

Mr Moore waited patiently. "You and Mr Hamm don't quite see eye to eye. It's a pity. He's a good teacher." He might be a good teacher, whatever that means, I thought, but he's not what I'd call a good person. A fair person. A kind person. Or even an OK person. I had more of an idea of what a good person was due to the number of bad persons in my life. 'Contrast and compare' as all the essay questions ask. I kind of smiled at the old Principal. What I was dying to tell him was the secret life of Mr Hamm—and the hot English Literature teacher, Ms Gerrard. They had this secret relationship that most of the school knew about or guessed. I'd had Ms Gerrard for Lit and was going to have her again in Year 11. What stuck in my throat was how she could be with an oaf like Hamm. I mean, she liked stories and ideas even when they came from my mouth. And she'd read John Morrison, so what she could see in old Hambone was beyond me. "Must both have really crap lives," was what Roxy came up with.

I realised Mr Moore was trying to have a chat, so I shook my head to get rid of the image of both of them naked, cavorting around in some bedroom. I tried hard to remember what he'd asked me. "What's going on in your life?" It's a hell of a question when you think about it. You can give the most vague, generalised responses or quickly get down to the nitty gritty which I only normally did with Roxy. Trouble with even a hint of the nitty gritty, you can find yourself falling down very deep holes which aren't anywhere near as nice and intriguing as the one Alice went down when she followed the white rabbit. If only my holes were filled with caterpillars smoking shisha, or tea parties or even the wacko queen ordering her soldiers to decapitate her supposed enemies. If only.

I went for somewhere in between. "Decided to do Year 11. Grandma's happy about that."

Mr Moore leant forward. "And how is your grandmother? You live with her, don't you?"

"Seems like I've lived with her all my life. Dunno what I'd do without her. She's going OK I guess. Although the doctor reckons she's got diabetes 2... and high blood pressure."

"Really? That's no good. Health is one of those things you take for granted when you're younger." Mr Moore got up, seemingly a bit agitated. He stood looking at a family photo on the bookshelf, the one I'd seen earlier on my first visit to his office. There were three people—him, someone who was probably his wife and a younger woman, in her mid-twenties.

"Yes," he mused, almost talking to himself, "you take a lot of things for granted... my wife, Jenny's her name, we were going to travel when I retired, see our daughter, Michelle, up on the Sunshine Coast, maybe Vietnam, or Paris..." He fell silent. I can usually deal with silence—I've had some in my time and I'm pretty silent myself—but I shifted in my chair and found looking at the glass top of the small coffee table the only place I could gaze at.

Mr Moore kept his silence going. I checked him out and hoped he wasn't crying.

"You can still go travelling, Mr Moore. Like if you retire sometime soon, you could take off... couldn't you?" My voice sounded imploring. I mean, what did I know? I was only seventeen, giving advice, making sympathetic murmurings to an old Principal who'd worked all his life, probably thinking for the last couple of years what kind of pleasure he could look forward to...

He took down the photo and looked at it. When he spoke, he spoke to the photo. "Ah, I don't know, son. Probably not. Jenny's been diagnosed with Alzheimer's. It's reasonably advanced... unfortunately."

A pall hung over the office. We could have been anywhere in the world and the pall would have remained, like a bank of grey clouds that could let loose its load any second. Alzheimer's. I knew only a skerrick of information about it, but when Mr Moore said the word it sounded like a thunderclap in the quiet hush of his office. Alzheimer's. Memory loss was what came to mind.

Mr Moore continued, like I wasn't there. He stared out the window, then back at the photo, then looked into the distance as though remembering something.

"A black wattle tree in our backyard came down the other week. Huge winds and we were out somewhere. When we came home there was the tree, slowly falling over. It looked like it was going to hit our power lines and our tiled roof but falling over ever so slowly. It was a pitch black night. We called Emergency Services, but they got there ten minutes late. By this time, our neighbours saw the emergency arrive and all the kerfuffle about the tree. By the time they'd left, me and Jenny and a couple of our neighbours sat around and talked about it all."

Mr Moore kept on talking, unaware of anything else. I sat patiently wondering if the old guy had Alzheimer's as well. "Well, anyway, the next morning I took Jenny her cup of tea and said, 'That was an adventure last night wasn't it?' Jenny looked at me and said, 'What do you mean?'"

I said, "Last night—when the tree took for ever to fall over. Remember, the emergency services came."

"What tree?" she asked.

Mr Moore stopped his story, looking at the framed photo but not really seeing it. I wanted to say something but as easy as words sometimes come to me, they didn't arrive. If my reply was a train arriving at the station, it hadn't even left the depot.

"She, I mean Jenny... Mrs Moore—couldn't remember anything? Not a bit?"

Mr Moore seemed relieved that I'd said something at least. He looked at me, almost surprised to find me sitting there.

"Not a bit," he sighed, placing the photo back in its place.

Chapter Five

Media camps at Riverside College were legendary. You had to be in Year 11 or have special permission to attend. I worried that some teacher might object to me going but really, the notion of me not being at school for a week gave some of them a sense of calm. I had changed a little since my junior years at the school but on some days it still didn't take much for me to be... well, just annoying even though I sat there saying nothing.

Roxy and I were definitely going—Roxy in particular couldn't contain her excitement. A whole week of film making, finding locations, shooting, editing was heaven to her. I wanted to go too but didn't have her passion for the world of celluloid. The chances of knocking up a story to film however did grab me. The reputation of the camp was never put into exact words but the rumours of lots of freedom, night parties in the rooms or on the beach, and not too much of 'do this, don't do that, what d'you think you're doing', made me salivate—drool might be a better word. The two teachers who ran it demanded a lot of what they called, 'self-direction', which was OK by me. I'd been self-directed most of my life, even when I had little or nothing to say about what was going on in my life. The two teachers were a couple, husband and wife, partners—whatever term takes your fancy. Stan and Izzy. Stan was short for Stanislav and Izzy short for Isabelle. Stan was a big Russian with thinning, smoky fair hair and a ponytail—probably too old for a bloody ponytail but with my different coloured hair styles who was I to judge? Isabelle apparently came from Egypt—saucer shaped eyes, like a middle eastern moon, and greying black hair that fell down to her arse. Both of them were so committed to their little film making department that nothing got in their way. I kind of respected that. I'd only ever had one run-in with these guys. In Year Ten I was fresh from a maths class with Hamm which had put me in the mood where I was hanging out to be sent to Mr Moore's office. I walked into Media and the first thing Stan says is, "Morrison I heard you write stories. When are we going to see them?"

I know, a perfectly innocent question, a reasonable enquiry, even friendly. So how did I respond: "Dunno where you heard that from Stan. Sounds like bullshit to me. Why would I bother spending my time doing that—like, that's about as stupid as people making little movies."

Yeah, I know. You don't go throwing garbage in people's faces when they look and sound like they're on your side. And you don't offend their passion, what lies at the heart of their being. But I did. After Hamm's class I either wanted someone to punch me or send me to Mr Moore. Neither of which he did. Stan took off his glasses, cleaning them on his T-shirt. I was ready for any response, the worst the better. The rest of the students waited for the execution. Stan looked at me, took one step towards me, put on his glasses and said, "Morrison. That's pathetic!" And that was it. To be honest, it was what I deserved and made me feel—just a bit pathetic.

The camp began on the Monday with all of us travelling by bus on the Sunday down to Senora. It was a sleepy little seaside town that hugged the coast of Westernport Bay. The camp was an array of long huts with dormitories, shower and toilet blocks, a big hall for meetings and eating and several rooms for all the filming and editing equipment. It was set next to a sad looking stretch of beach covered with kilometres of thick cobwebs of dark green seaweed. Between the camp and the beach ran a fetid, tidal creek with a recently built wooden footbridge.

The first night I realised why the camp had a certain reputation. As long as you didn't shove it in Stan or Izzy's faces or do something really stupid—like go into the little shopping centre and start doing a striptease, which apparently had been done in the past—as long as you did your drinking and smoking out of sight, they didn't care. What they did care about was you taking the camp seriously and producing a short film by the end of the camp. We had to work in groups, writing, shooting, directing, editing. On that first night, Roxy and I sat way down the beach, listening to the lap of the diminutive grey waves when a small figure loomed out of the darkness. He sat down next to us without a word.

"Terry, mate. Where did you come from?"

"Me mum drove me down. Didn't trust me to take the bus with all you older kids. She's gone now. Had a talk to Izzy." Terry's voice was as soft as the waves.

"How come you're here. You're not old enough are you?" Roxy asked, slapping at a mossie zeroing in on her bare arms.

"They let me come. Think my home group teacher, Rosario, had a word. She knows I love movies and that, so they let me come. Thought it might help me."

"Help you become a drinker and a smoker, you mean," I said. Memories of the never-ending title fights between Rosario and Morrison in Year Eight tumbled around. "So Ms Rosario, looked after you, eh?"

Little Terry chuckled. "Yep. Heard you and she didn't get along too well. Anyway here I am. Lucky m'mum saw nothing of all this," he said sweeping his arm down the beach where lights from phones and small fires stretched along the shore. Music slipped its way through the layers of cold night air. "I heard her ask Izzy where all the kids were. I think Izzy said all the kids were either sleeping or preparing for their week's filming. Pretty funny, eh?"

Roxy ruffled Terry's sandy hair. "We have to make a film in groups. You can be with us if you like."

Terry kicked sand up with his feet. "Thanks. Might as well. Can't imagine any of the others wanting me."

The next day Stan set out our tasks. Our movies could only be between five and ten minutes long, they had to tell some kind of a story, and somewhere, somehow our films had to say something. "The most important thing for any kind of story is that you have to have something to say." I'm sure John Morrison would have agreed with that, otherwise what's the point? Stan waited for questions, but none came. "Apart from a story we can all understand"—Stan gave the group of stoners a good hard look—"if you're going to use dialogue, make it believable. It has to be close to real talk but different. Like a balance between real and giving it meaning." Most of the kids were yawning and thinking about how they could stuff around for a few days and still come up with a film.

"Anybody got anything to add?"

A sheet of silence was thrown over the crowd of film makers extraordinaire. Stan was about to wrap it up when a tiny faint voice spoke up. "Yeah, you wouldn't want your script to be full of the way people actually speak." The rest of us looked around. Whoever it was wasn't making themselves too obvious.

"Hello Terry," Stan said. "Glad you could make it. Why do you say that mate?"

The rest of the group's eyes finally found little Terry. "Well, y'know when A talks to B, A prattles on, then B talks to A and B prattles on, then A goes again but A hardly ever responds to what B said and when B replies and has his say, B almost never responds to what A says. You know what I mean?"

Stan and Izzie exchanged looks, with Izzie laughing out loud. "That's a very cool observation, Terry," Izzie said. "Did all of you get that?"

Roxy and I sure as hell got it. Like I said about little Terry, he had a brain and a mouth to show it. I checked out the stoners—they were looking at Terry like he was a prophet or something, while the rest smirked or shook their heads patronisingly.

Stan told us to organise ourselves into groups of four and get working. Me and Roxy grabbed hold of Terry. The stoners looked like drafting him, like they might simply put Terry in front of a camera and let him rave. Not likely. We wanted the boy genius. But we only had three. Most people had found themselves in a group and there were a few left-over, lost souls who would always be picked last for the school yard cricket game. When I thought about it, most of the crowd had its full complement of tossers. There was Ivan in his dark glasses, cap pulled low over his eyes; some girl dressed in black, complete with white makeup and looking oh so bored daahhlings; another girl, probably called Tiffany or Sasha with long flowing blond hair, and a green velvet dress that fell over her bare feet; and next to her was her boyfriend, George who also had long flowing fair hair, and was fond of wearing diaphanous silk shirts. You could guarantee their film would consist of long, blurred shots of his girlfriend running over dunes or looking wistfully out to sea. All of them could see their names in lights, their names on the backs of director's chairs, limousines and red carpets. Even the up-themselves media students who constantly hung it on commercial movies because 'how could the movie be any good if it was so popular?' had the same pathetic dreams.

I was lost in my own enjoyment of dissecting those around us when Terry said, "What about him?" I looked at Roxy. Talk about good ideas coming from the mouths of babes. For there on the outskirts stood Petticoat Boy. Talk about obvious. We were already the group of misfits but having Petticoat Boy would seal the deal. Roxy sauntered over to him, "Hey mate, wanna join us?" He took one look at us and burst out laughing—"Perfect," he smiled. His name was Marcus, from a Greek family and for his first day at the camp he'd chosen a black petticoat which he wore over a T-shirt and jeans. "Wonder how the petticoats went down with his family?" I asked Roxy. "No problem as what to buy him for Christmas," she giggled.

So there we were, the four most unlikely Musketeers. Roxy was going to be the director and camera—no ifs, buts or maybes. All of us would have to come up with the story and anything left over, like lights, mics, acting would have to be covered by me, Terry and Pettic... Marcus. We could do the movie using a phone, but Roxy wasn't having any of that. "When we've got access to good digital cameras, that's how we'll do it. And there's no way I'm not using a Blackmagic when we've got one to use."

I'd heard about this camera from Roxy before who said it was the Lamborghini of movie cameras. The fact that the school only had one of these beauties and that there were six movies being shot at the one time didn't faze her at all. I knew she'd get it—none of the up themselves 'directors' had a chance (in truth, they were just a tiny bit scared of her) and the stoners probably would've shrugged and said, 'yeah, cool Roxy, whatever.' Terry opened his mouth to challenge her but one look from the DIRECTOR made him think twice. Roxy was like that—she'd thought the whole thing through, things none of us other Musketeers had dreamt of. On top of that she could be a total bossy bitch which had led to some disagreements between me and her. The thing that bugged me was that she was often right. I couldn't have cared less what kind of camera we'd use, my mind was already full of what kind of story, what story was worth telling. I tracked through some of John Morrison's stories—some of them you would have wondered why he bothered writing. Old grumpy union officials who turned out to be helpful blokes; a war of flowers and gardens between two sisters and their gardeners; arguments between friends over winning lottery tickets; one story about a man waiting for his bus in the Dandenong Ranges, witnessing birds and ants and nature bustling all around him. Nothing really came to mind, nothing popped up saying, 'write me, write me.'

Roxy and Terry went off to book the equipment and to see what else we might need for our shoot the next day, which only gave us a day and a night to come up with a story that was worth the telling. Me and Petticoat Boy—I had to stop that but years of knowing him as that and not as 'Marcus' was difficult to drop. I explained this to him as we wandered off to the beach to see what ideas might materialise. He laughed when I told him. "Call me Petticoat Boy if you want. Everybody else does. One time someone called out, 'Marcus' and I turned around to see who Marcus was. Funny eh?"

The beach was less romantic in the daylight. Plastic rings from six packs, bits and pieces of blue twine tangled in the seaweed, a few dead puffer fish, their spikes still erect and threatening, lost thongs, kid's spades left behind in the marron grass, rainbow circles of oil looped on the sand, and the ubiquitous pairs of discarded, half-buried jocks. We walked for some time along this stretch until we came to a small sand hill where we perched ourselves. Marcus breathed in the sea air. Me too—the coolness, saltiness, the fresh sticky air. It was possible for me to remain wordless for a long time which I was normally happy to use as a moat around my Morrison castle, but Petticoat deserved more than that.

"So, any ideas for our little movie, Morrison?" he asked.

I picked up a smooth stick of driftwood and doodled in the sand. "Nah, not yet. But what I do know is that often as not your story is right under your nose. Just gotta be ready for it when it comes knocking." Marcus grinned. "So where's the Morrison bit come from?"

Not many had the balls to ask me that and when they did it gave me so many opportunities. 'Named after my great-great-grandfather who died in World War One; found it written on a note in a bottle washed up onshore; I used to be a girl called Molly but I'm trans, so I called myself after my surgeon; I'm Mr Hamm's lovechild—he named me after his plumber… '

I relented and told Marcus the truth. And when I thought about it, my name change really wasn't all that much of a big deal, which made me realise that you don't have to stray too far from the norm, the accepted ways of behaving for others to see your actions as a big deal—weird and hard to deal with.

He smiled and said, "Maybe I could change my name officially to Petticoat."

I grinned back. "Now that would look excellent on your résumé. Especially if you were going for a job as a builder's labourer."

We sat there for some time, with only the lapping of the miniature waves and some plovers with their haunting cries for company. I wasn't sure what was going through Petticoat's mind but mine was working bloody hard, cranking and grinding its way through possibilities. I remembered a short anecdote by John Morrison on the never ending search for the right story. A friend of his, Mary had written a story about two women and one man living together in a lighthouse. The trouble was that the women both loved the one man. Reading between the lines it was obvious that Morrison thought the story was a load of tripe. So he starts asking questions to Mary if she had ever lived in a lighthouse, chatted to any lighthouse keeper, ever investigated how lighthouses actually function and so on. Of course to every question Mary replied, "No." Then John Morrison takes another tack. He asks her what her job is. Mary worked in Myers, a big department store in the city. Before long Mary can't stop gabbling on how she's the boss of a number of shop assistants, how they all bring their problems of things like pregnancy, boyfriends cheating on them, engagements, abortions—to her. Mary also talked for ages about the customers, the snobs, the weirdos, even the old homeless guy who regularly sneaks handfuls of nuts from the Nut Bar then moves onto the perfumery counter where he tries out a number of testers. On and on she goes until John Morrison interrupts her and says, "Mary, with all these stories under your nose, why on earth did you write about two women and a man in a lighthouse, something you know absolutely nothing about."

Marcus sat there quiet as I could be. My brain was in overdrive, so much so that I wondered if he could hear all the clanking and whirring. I kept on mulling over that idea of stories being under your nose but still nothing leapt out of the water.

Marcus stood up and stretched and did some yoga poses—somehow that didn't surprise me. After five minutes of stretching, leaning, bending and breathing he stared into the now grey metallic sea. "Y'know, when I wonder about who I am, what I am, what other people think of me, I wonder about how I... me... how we all came about. Not just me and petticoats and you with your life and changing your name but going way back to what made us like we are, who we are." He took a deep breath from the rolling deep.

Now to most people, Marcus' waffling on would be just that, waffle. But his little philosophising pressed some buttons for me. I wandered down to the water's edge and stood with Petticoat Boy staring at... what? Were we expecting Jesus to emerge from the brine in his board shorts and flippers to tell us the origin of life? A Pacific gull passed overhead and landed on the water, gently floating, slipping up and over the crests. Then, as it often happens, the idea crashed all around me, and swirled over my feet. No more hard clanking and drudge, just a white hot idea, a beginning that, when I wrote, would unfold like clean sheets.

Marcus looked at me strangely, like maybe I'd been talking out loud.

"Gotta go, mate. Let Roxy know I've got an idea and I've gone off to write it down." Marcus smiled and nodded. I found a small room in one of the dormitories that used to be an office. I slapped my writing pad on a table and started to write. As I began I hoped that it would turn into something rather than just remain as a good idea.

CHAPTER SIX

Film Synopsis:

Deserted beach. A cool day with the threat of rain. Wind scurries up the sand. A small boy wanders along the shoreline, dragging a stick behind him. He seems familiar with the beach like it's a place he visits often. The boy has similar physical characteristics to the central character in the film, Stormboy—kind of innocent and unkempt. He continues walking and sees a figure, very indistinct, in the distance. The figure sits on a small sand dune. The boy stops, looks and continues. He is interested in the figure but perhaps a little wary. After all, this beach is the boy's playground and it's usually empty of other human beings.

The boy walks on, dragging his stick, stopping every now and then to check on the person in the distance. As he gets closer the figure becomes a man, then, a rather old man. The boy finally reaches the man and stops, looking at him. The man is dressed in a white shirt with the sleeves rolled up to his elbows. He is barefooted, wearing dark grey pants with the trouser legs rolled up to his calves. The man stares out to sea, almost completely still. After a minute he notices the boy, nods and smiles at him. The boy thinks about joining the old guy but decides against it and walks away.

The next day, the boy follows his trail of yesterday. He looks for the man again, but he doesn't seem to be there. The boy walks on and when he checks again, there's the old bloke in the distance but now he's sitting on the beach, closer to the incoming tide. This time when the boy reaches him, they both gaze at each other. The kid asks the man what he's doing which is met by silence. The kid asks him again and the bloke replies that he's not sure. The kid questions the old guy again about why he's sitting there. Eventually he says that he's not at all sure why he's sitting on a deserted beach day after day. All he knows is that he's not sure where he's from and that maybe the beach will provide an answer. The boy listens politely but as he gets up to leave he notices some scarring on the side of the old guy's neck.

The following day much the same thing happens. The boy has grown in confidence and asks the bloke where he thinks he's from and is he lost or something else. The man can't answer any of the questions and appears to become more confused. The boy studies his face and notices that the scarring has turned into three or four distinct scars, about three centimetres long on the side of his neck.

Next day the same thing happens although the man seems to be more agitated, to the point where he stands up and walks a few feet into the water. The boy asks him what he's doing to which the man simply shrugs his shoulders and shakes his head disconsolately. Then he says that he has no real idea who he is and once again, no idea where he's from but he thinks he's where he should be. The kid walks into the water mainly to check out the scarring. This time they are clearly defined, almost like crude lips, slightly open, dark red on the outside, rose pink on the inside.

The final day comes, and the boy can't see the man on the beach nor on the small dune. He quickens his pace, almost runs to where they used to sit on the wet sand. The man is nowhere to be seen. The kid is in a panic, looking everywhere around him. Finally he sees him, walking into the sea, up to his chest but still going. The boy calls out to him. The man stops, turns to the shore. From where he is, the kid can clearly see the openings on the man's neck. The kid's face is like one big question mark. The old guy smiles, waves and can just be heard saying as he sinks into the swell of the ocean, "It's OK. I know where I come from. I know where I belong."

I had no idea how long I'd been writing but it felt like the words had simply tumbled onto the page. I liked what I'd written—at least I thought it was pretty good. But that didn't mean the others would take to it. Roxy of course was my main concern.

But I needn't have worried. "Wow, Morrison. This is great. Can't say I understand it, but it'll film well." Both Marcus and Terry agreed although neither were quite sure what the hell the story meant. To tell you the truth, I didn't either but figured it was intriguing enough so I decided I'd remain dark and mysterious about it all and wait to see what others got from it. Of course I couldn't wait for the wanky film makers to put forward their theories to which I couldn't wait to thoughtfully stroke my chin and say, "Hmmm, that's interesting."

Director Roxy did have one good question: "OK. It's obvious we got Terry for the role of the little kid, but do you reckon we can have Stan made up to look old? Or what about you Petticoat, reckon we can make you look about eighty?"

"Only if the old guy can wear a petticoat," Marcus replied. Terry and I cracked up, but Roxy had her I-am-a-serious-director face on and didn't join in. We asked Stan if he was up to it, but he figured he'd be moving around between the different movies being shot. "I'll be the last resort if nothing else turns up," he said.

We hoped something else would turn up. As a small kid living in one of the stream of run-down derelict houses my mother and I lived in ('lived in' was hardly what we were doing—'existing' doesn't even come close) I constantly hoped that 'something else would turn up'. One place, I think it was a lonely, deserted farmhouse next to a roundabout where at night semis, cattle trucks and tankers roared, sending shadows and stripes of light monstering across my room. I hoped that something else would turn up because I knew what I had wasn't any good. I didn't need any comparisons in my young life to know that. Sure my mother gave me kisses now and then, usually the early stages of being drunk as a lord or whacked out of her brain, but they never made me feel treasured or loved—just a thing she thought that mothers were supposed to do.

Four of us found a room with two double bunks, and we went to bed that night, all thinking about what might turn up. And yes—you guessed it. Something did. But not one of us had any inkling of something being presented to us on a platter. Although the platter would take some effort in getting it to the table.

It was customary for Mr Moore to visit the film camp for a day. I guess he liked escaping school as much as us. And he was no fool—he'd heard the rumours about the 'film camp'! Before he arrived there'd been a big clean-up, supervised by Stan and Izzy. Cans, bottles, butts and used condoms filled six bins which were taken into the ti-tree bush that bordered the camp. Terry couldn't stop laughing and saying "Gees this is funny!" which was very uncool (although the stoners pissed themselves laughing every time he said it) but he was only thirteen, so we felt protective of him.

Ms Rosario drove Mr Moore down—so she could see how Terry was going, I suppose. When she realised that he was in our group, her eyes popped, becoming as big as her pregnant belly. I saw her talking with Izzy and surreptitiously nodding in my direction. But good old Izzy seemed to calm her down and Terry seemed as happy as she'd ever seen him in class, so nothing was said or done and little Terry continued to work in the group that reputedly had as one of its members a well-known axe murderer, cocaine dealer, child molester and destroyer of classroom peace.

Mr Moore spotted me in the dining room eating our lunch of hot dogs and fruit. I saw him look at me, briefly while Stan chatted away with him and Ms Rosario. Stan usually ate like a peasant—huge mouthfuls of food in between a stream of information about how the camp was going. I'm sure that Mr Moore was interested while bits of half-masticated hot dog flew from Stan's overactive mouth. When Mr Moore saw me he gave this small smile and a subtle nod. I gave him one back in return. It was strange that we didn't go up to each other and say things like 'Hello' and 'long time since you've been outside my office' and so on. For a start it hadn't been a long time since I'd been outside his office—I'd had a recent stint there due to a misunderstanding between me and Ms Cottrell, the old English teacher. She'd told me to pick up some rubbish, mainly because I was allegedly the closest one to it and she never had much time for me anyway. As a rule, picking up chip bags and orange peel doesn't worry me too much, but it was the way she asked—the way she told me to do it. When you've lived the kind of life I've lived, the smallest insult or what you perceive to be rude is something that can trigger responses that's usually slightly over the top. And I'd had a gutful of being told to pick up bottles, paper, and plastic whenever I was within fifty meters of it.

"You mean these pieces of rubbish, Miss or that one over there?" I smiled, pointing at a tiny ball of crumpled tinfoil next to a bin down the corridor.

Ms Cottrell put on this tired grimace and said, "Well Morrison, I've heard you're a smart young man. What do you think I meant?"

"Thank you Miss but quite frankly I'm not sure. I guess it depends on what piece of rubbish is likely to spread disease— or maybe one offends the eye more than the other." Ms Cottrell slowly began to boil. Her small plump body seemed to be puffing up like those tiny frogs that pump up their bodies to fool predators about their actual size. "Perhaps you could tell me, Miss. You've been a teacher for a long time— which bit is the right one to pick up?"

Ms Cottrell stood silent, her obvious heart condition now in full play.

"Morrison!!!!!" she shrieked.

I dropped to the floor and scurried around like a whipped dog, more like a hunchback on all fours, not only collecting bits of rubbish but also seizing wrappers and cans and paper from kids who were still eating and drinking who all began yelling at me. But I didn't stop—I raced all over the place grabbing anything and everything that could be labelled as rubbish, saying to the pissed off kids, "I'm sorry. I'm sorry. Don't blame me. Miss Cottrell wants ALL THE RUBBISH GONE!!" In the midst of the ensuing chaos I finally stopped my antics and presented the bin to the English teacher, placed it at her feet, bowed and walked off.

Of course by the time I was in my English Lit class, the word had got around, and Ms Gerrard was called out of the room by Cottrell. And so I found myself once more wending my way to Mr Moore's office.

Which brings me back to why we didn't display the fact that we had spent some time together over the years, albeit in his office while being 'punished'. In the first place, it has never been cool to be 'friends' with a teacher, or for that matter, with anyone in a position of authority. And teachers being mates with students is a definite no-no. For all kinds of reasons. It was a little-known fact that Mr Moore knew me reasonably well, but it was a well-known fact that I was and could be a real pain in the arse. Somehow the mixture didn't go well. However, while I was eating with Roxy and the other two she caught me giving Mr Moore a nod. "Why don't you go and say hello to your special friend?" she mocked.

I gave her a look in return, which I reserved for stupid comments. "Oh sure, just rock up and say hi Mr Moore me old mate and you too Ms Rosario, long time no see. Gees I wish we could both go back to the good ol' days when you hated me, and I made your life a misery. So happy you're having a kid—maybe I could babysit sometime."

Before Roxy could come up with a good comeback, the other three went silent and there was Mr Moore standing in front of me.

"Hello Morrison. Heard you were on the camp. Stan tells me you four are working on a film together."

Roxy, Terry and Petticoat Boy went silent, but all nodded like those stupid clowns at the show where you put ping pong balls in their mouths. In that minute, I seriously wished I'd had some ping pong balls.

"Er, yeah, sure Mr Moore. Doing a film. Yep, that's right. Making a movie." I felt like I'd become one of those clowns, white faced and big red lips, choking on a little white ball." I glanced at Roxy. "But Roxy is the Director. She knows all about it." Roxy kicked me in the shins but suddenly, out of the blue, little Terry gave a quick look at me and said, in his rapid fire mousey voice. "I'll tell you Mr Moore. We'll wait all day to hear it from them. It's about this little kid who comes across an old man sitting on the beach looking out to sea. But he has no clue why he's there. The kid keeps on coming back over the next few days and the old bloke still doesn't know why he's sitting on the beach. Meanwhile the old man has got these things on the sides of his neck which seem to grow more each day. Anyway, on the final day the kid can't find the bloke but then sees him in the water wading into the sea."

Mr Moore smiled and polished an apple on the sleeve of his neat grey cardigan. "So why is he walking into the sea, Terry?" Mr Moore had given up on getting any sense out of me and Roxy.

"Umm, we're not sure but the old guy reckons that now he knows where he comes from."

Mr Moore looked at his shiny apple. "So you're leaving it up to the audience to work it out?"

The four of us looked at each other. "Who came up with this story?" Roxy, Terry and Marcus swivelled and stared at me. I looked down at the table—there were some grains of salt and pepper that looked awfully important.

"You, eh Morrison?" He laughed quietly, almost to himself, then walked off, chuckling, shaking his head. There was dead silence at the table. Petticoat Boy turned to Terry, "Good summary, Terry." More silence. Then Roxy quietly said, "To think we've been looking for an old guy for the movie." Big light bulbs, popping and exploding above all our heads. Big smiles. A few high fives. More silence.

"You're going to have to ask him, Morrison."

"Whaaaat?! No. No not me. Why not you Roxy? You are the DIRECTOOOR after all."

Little Terry just shook his head and Petticoat patted me on the back and said, "Off you go genius. Can't get out of this one."

Finally I stood up and said, "Thanks a lot," and went off to find the old guy.

I found him standing at the crappy little bridge made out of offcuts and old trunks of ti-tree. He was staring into the weedy creek with fingers of slime waving in the sludge. He seemed to be in a world of his own—something that we all love at times, although I needed that world more than most. Mr Moore looked up, glad to see me.

"G'day Mr Moore."

"Hello again, Morrison." He was quieter than usual.

"Getting some fresh air, Sir?"

He looked down at the creek, full of gunge and gloop. "I doubt if I'll find it down there. But the sea air is invigorating."

I remained standing there like a full-on dickhead. "You like the outdoors, Mr Moore?"

"Love the outdoors, Morrison. Used to go camping with Jenny—Mrs Moore—all the time. Did a spot of river fishing." He looked up at me. "Used to but not for a while now. Every now and then she remembers a camping trip from the past—but not often. I was told that getting her to reminisce would help her memory, but it doesn't seem to work too often—maybe every now and then." He heaved a sigh that came from the deep. Subterranean. Unsettling. I shifted uncomfortably, studying the green fingers in the water.

"What's up Morrison? I know you're a quiet one but you're beginning to worry me."

As if the old guy didn't have enough on his plate. I plunged in. "Well, you know the story I wrote for our film. We've got everything kind of organised, Roxy's filming, Terry's the little kid, Petticoat—Marcus—will be hanging onto reflectors and rain hoods and I'll be the general 'gofer' but we need the old— the elderly, y'know the guy sitting on the beach..."

Mr Moore broke into soft laughter which continued for some time. OK it was a dumb thing to ask. He's near retiring, his wife has no memory and who knows, may not even remember him on some days and here's Ms Rosario's favourite nightmare asking for a favour. A big favour.

Mr Moore finally stopped his chortling, straightened up and giving his left knee a vigorous rub said, "Well better show me where the action's taking place. Let me think about it."

We walked down along the shore. An icy wind cut through our clothes. I pointed out where the movie was going to be shot. He stood there, his polished black shoes sinking into wet sand, looking at the first swell of the small waves. "You got insurance?" he asked, straight-faced.

"Eh?" I said.

"That's what horses eat, son. I think you mean, 'Pardon?' And what about the pay scale? Do I get more because it's cold and dangerous?"

Now I was completely confused. "Pardon? Dangerous?"

"Well just look at the water. It could sweep you out to sea before you knew it."

I started to explain that the water couldn't sweep a baby out to sea, but Mr Moore burst out laughing. And I mean fall-down laughing. So Mr Moore had me good and proper. I searched for some face-saving explanation or maybe a smart-arse crack, but nothing arose and anyway, Mr Moore was laughing too hard to hear me. I'd never heard him laugh much and certainly not as raucous as that. I allowed myself a smile, but I could feel my face burning. I can laugh at myself occasionally (which my grandma considers a virtue) but old Mr Moore taking the piss out of me...

His hilarity finally calmed down. Mr Moore put his hand on my shoulder saying, "See, Morrison, I've been taking lessons from you." His face said it all. "But don't worry I won't be spreading this around the staffroom." He was still smiling like a Cheshire cat when he asked, "Well, OK Morrison. As long as you think I can do it. But it will mean I'll have to stay overnight. I'll check with Ms Rosario and Stan and Izzy but pretty sure it'll be OK. Have to phone Jenny's carer too—sometimes she can stay overnight." He stared at me. "And just as long as this piece of acting doesn't lead to a Hollywood career—I have to think of my reputation." The last bit was said with a smirk. Fair dinkum, the old guy was full of small surprises. And maybe a smidgin of smartarseness.

As soon as he walked off I realised what his decision would mean. The Principal would be staying overnight (and apparently Ms Rosario as well) so the unspoken message was that the Media Camp merry-making would be put on hold. When Stan announced that afternoon the changed circumstances and why it had occurred there was a polite silence. In fact the silence was so silent it sounded like the roar from eighty thousand at the MCG. If someone had dropped a pin it would've sounded like a roadworks jackhammer at four in the morning.

The stoners blinked and the nouveau directors glared at our little group, particularly at me. Somehow this gave me some bizarre satisfaction. Why, I am not sure but just giving the shits to most of them amused me. It didn't worry me about the dope (I was not a virgin in this area), nor the drinking (although the latter did give me flashbacks of episodes from my childhood) nor those lucky enough to have sex—for some very peculiar reason I felt protective of Mr Moore. If any of the other movie makers had made one crappy comment about him spoiling their fun I would've made them 'rethink their attitude' as I'd been told to do many times. In fact I probably would've sent them to sit outside the Principal's office.

Next morning Roxy was shaking the hell out of me telling me to wake up. It was 6am. I am not an early morning person, and Petticoat wasn't either. "Come on you guys. Mr Moore's already up and wondering where we are." OK that was enough to drag us out of our sleeping bags and chuck on some clothes and stumble over to the dining room. Little Terry was already there, chatting to Mr Moore, chirping along with all the other birds singing their morning song. Both of them were holding hot cups of tea, tendrils of steam in the cold air. Nobody else was up. Fortunately, Mr Moore and Ms Rosario had retired early the night before, so the party, although somewhat muted had continued.

Roxy already had the Blackmagic camera, hoods, reflectors. We weren't worrying about makeup and Terry and Mr Moore's clothes were perfect as they were.

"Will it be alright with you Mr Moore if we get you to roll your sleeves up and your pants as well?" Roxy asked. Mr Moore nodded and smiled. He seemed happy—and nervous.

"And my shoes?" he asked.

"Oh yeah forgot that," said Roxy. "Maybe keep them on for the first couple of scenes and then when we get to the end they should be off."

It was then I realised that the old guy would end up in the water. Like, right in the water. The others hadn't thought about that aspect. I had no idea whether Mr Moore had thought about it. As we traipsed over the little bridge and onto the sand, I sidled up to him. "Mr Moore. Can I talk to you about something?" He nodded. "Umm... you do realise that in the last scene you're in the water? Like most of you in the water. Like all your clothes will be soaked... you'll need a change... and anyway... you're..."

"An old man." Mr Moore finished my thought. I felt as though I'd insulted him and embarrassed myself.

"You can stop worrying, Morrison. I talked to Stan last night. He raised it with me—pretty much the way you did, actually—and he's got some old clothes." He looked at me and put his hand on my shoulder. "And don't worry too much. I'm not likely to drop dead on the spot." He began to walk away but stopped. "Anyway, just imagine how good your film would be if you captured my death." I stood stock still, studying his face, searching for any trace of sarcasm. Mr Moore walked off to join the others, but as he did so he glanced over his shoulder at me, a wicked smile all over his face. What a smartarse!

And so the great little movie began. It went on all day, the chill wind blowing sand and Roxy the DIRECTOR giving orders to all and sundry, especially to me: "Get a water bottle. Help Marcus hold the reflectors. Remind Terry of his lines. Come on Morrison, where's that tape I asked for? Help Mr Moore roll up his trousers. We haven't time for lunch—get some salad rolls. Jesuuus Morrison, where've you been? I thought you only went to the toilet—what you been doing? Writing a short story?"

On and on it went and if it hadn't been my mate-without-benefits, Roxy, and Mr Moore's involvement (and of course the fact I wrote the script) I would've given her some Morrison treatment. However the strangest aspect of the whole afternoon was that slowly and gradually an audience grew. Ms Rosario, Steve and Izzy and then most of the other kids wound up strung along the crest of the small dunes, watching the story unfold. And mostly in silence. The thing is that all students and most teachers (and parents as well but my knowledge of that aspect was severely limited) saw school Principals as 'people of authority', all cut from the same cloth, conservative and not to be messed with. Now, as a rule I'd say that could well be true and until I met Mr Moore I would've gone along with it. But as grandma says, 'don't judge a book by its cover'. Which is not the best saying because most of us, most of the time, do exactly that. So our 'audience' watched as their ideas about school Principals slipped away as every tiny wave ebbed back into the sea. Some of them would have enjoyed seeing Roxy bossing me around (I caught Ms Rosario smirking) but on the whole they couldn't help being intrigued.

The small number of spoken lines helped, with Terry and Mr Moore mainly relying on walking, sitting and facial expressions for their acting debut. Everything went more or less according to plan. But then the final scene arrived. We had an offer from one of the girls who I'd disparaged earlier—the girl dressed in black, complete with white makeup and looking oh so bored daahhlings—she'd do the makeup for the marks on Mr Moore's neck. The finished product astounded me and not just because they looked so real—it was more because I'd judged a book by its cover. Doesn't pay to do that too often. And I should know seeing I'd suffered from it most of my life. I remember a snapshot of my life when my mother thought she'd be a 'good mother' and managed to get me into a kindergarten in one of the places we stayed in for longer than a month. When I arrived in thin hand-me-downs, skinny, pale, with big eyes that looked hungry for anything, most of the kids steered clear of me while the Kindy teachers tried to over-compensate which set me apart even more. They needn't have tried too much. I was out of there within three weeks, an eventful three weeks which included my mother forgetting (maybe) to collect me on a few occasions.

Our makeup artist was surprisingly called Lucy (not Claudia or Tiffany) and went about her work like a professional. The way she interacted with Mr Moore was kind and friendly. Mr Moore for his part went along with the whole deal, ignoring Lucy's own Goth, ghost-like made-up face. What I liked was that she 'got' the movie. She stood next to me while the second last scene was shot and then moved in to turn the 'wounds' into gills.

Now came the time for Mr Moore to enter the water. The old bloke didn't skip a beat, taking off his socks and shoes, removing his watch and walking into the water. This was the scene that would make the movie. I could see Roxy tensing up. She'd simply taken off her jeans and stood in the water as well, with just her knickers on. Good ol' Roxy. She didn't give a stuff. Although I had an inkling she was aware of Lucy chatting to me...

This was when Mr Moore's character realised why he'd been sitting looking out to sea. It was as if his memory had returned. The water was obviously freezing, arriving at this shore via the Antarctic and the Southern Ocean. The chill of the water was clearly affecting Roxy and Mr Moore, both in mood and communication. The DIRECTOR stood in the water trying to get the old fella to look slightly confused but clear about what he was about to do. Mr Moore clearly found this to be too contradictory but each time he queried Roxy all she could do was repeat herself, which only led to more confusion. The gang on the hill watched with bated breath wondering if Roxy was only going to be satisfied if her actor actually wept and drowned. Matters were becoming as tense as a Mr Hamm/Morrison confrontation.

Lucy turned to me and said, "Why don't you get down there and help him out. You know him." A slight fear of Roxy was overcome by my compassion for Mr Moore. "Hey, Rox. Hang on a minute. Let Mr Moore get out of the water for a minute. I think I can explain."

Roxy was so bound up in her own prison of imagination she seemed startled when I called out to her from the shore. Little Terry still sat on the sand, obediently following orders. Finally she nodded and waded ashore as did Mr Moore. She hung around as I grabbed a big blanket from Stan and wrapped it around Mr Moore. When he stopped shivering he gave me a wan smile as if to say that he hoped he wasn't stuffing up. I squatted next to him and spoke as quietly as I could. "Mr Moore... Sir. We better get this over with before you die of hypothermia. Listen, what, and I hope you don't mind me telling you, but what Roxy is saying is that she has to capture the feelings you have as you enter the water, like you can remember where you come from and... probably happy to be going back."

He nodded at me while staring at the sand. "Quite a few people up there looking, eh Morrison?" He paused. "Hope I'm not ruining your movie." Pause. "I'm not looking like an idiot am I?" I had a wild impulse to hug the guy which you may have understood by now that that's something that is not in my DNA.

"Definitely not, Mr Moore. And Roxy doesn't think so either, do you Roxy?"

Roxy shook her head emphatically, a bit too much to be convincing. I looked at Mr Moore, the sand, Roxy, Terry, Petticoat, the line on the hill—out at sea and then it hit me. I moved closer to Mr Moore, and in a voice only the salty water could hear, I said, "Hope you don't mind, Mr Moore but I think I know what could help you and I hope you won't be offended." He smiled. "Well, y'know your wife, Mrs Moore."

"Yes I'm pretty sure I do," he grinned. At least his sense of recently acquired smartarse humour was returning.

"Well it's like her memory isn't too good, like it's going. This guy, your character has been sitting on a beach wondering why he's there, what he's doing there. A bit like Mrs Moore. But when it finally hits him he seems relieved, like not completely sure but happy to begin the journey back to where he comes from. Like when Mrs Moore might remember something, like from that photo you got in your office. She might get just enough of a spark that makes her happy in that moment."

Mr Moore sat for a minute or two, dribbling sand through his fingers. His eyes welled up, but only so Roxy, Terry and I could see. He wrapped the blanket around his head to cover the wiping away of tears. Then he stood up, discarded the blanket, scuffed the sand off his hands and said, "OK Director, ready."

The scene was a blast. Like unbelievable. Applause from the sand dunes. Thumbs up from Stan and Izzie. A big smile from Ms Rosario to all of us—including me. Amazing. Mr Moore had somehow helped our little movie kind of make sense. And then Stan came down with another blanket and walked the hypothermic movie star back to the camp and a hot shower. Seagulls wheeling. Fading sunlight. Grey waves rocking on the gentle night sea.

CHAPTER SEVEN

The next couple of months went ahead as usual although every now and then someone would bring up Mr Film Star Moore. But it was mainly kept to the kids on the Media camp plus a few others. I'm not sure why it didn't rush around the school like a spot fire. I could only guess that most knew that they'd witnessed something pretty special and had kind of joined the club that felt protective of the old guy. And for some very weird reason it annoyed me. I mean, wasn't it me who got him to do the movie? And it was because of me that he gave it a go? And what did any of the others know about Mr Moore? Nothing. And I sure as hell wasn't about to spill my guts on anything I knew or kind-of-knew about Mr Moore. Looking back from my vantage point, I guess I was jealous of my—whatever it was—between me and Mr Moore.

The student film festival would be held at the end of the year at the local, trendy little theatre in Ballantyne. By that time I'd hoped that 'wasn't-Moore-bloody-fantastic' hype would've died down. What did die down for a month after the camp was me getting sent to Moore's office. Apparently my presence in class wasn't as rocky as it used to be. Teachers began treating me differently—well, that didn't apply to Mrs Jacobs, Ms Cottrell nor Mr Hamm. Even if they experienced any change in me they would have thought that I was up to some mysterious plan to bring the school down or, at the very least, introduce a new Corona virus to teachers and students alike. Anyway, some teachers thought they should smile at me more often, ask me how I was going, not give me a hard time if I turned up late. Punctuality wasn't a strong point of mine and why would it be? All I can remember about time when I was a little fella was that it dragged, or promises were made about something or other that were never kept, never came to fruition. Time for me in those years staggering through life was that it was a heavy load. It didn't pay for me to think what might lie ahead or what I had come from—to be honest, in those days I don't think I knew what day it was, much less the hour. I was in the present and to my little tacker brain nothing else promised anything. Some Buddhists might think I'd achieved some Zen moment where the only thing that matters is that specific moment—a moment that's supposed to be swaddled in peace, serenity, calmness—but my experience with time was nothing like that. Even as a very small child I knew time was at best, disappointing.

So why wasn't I driving teachers mad and vice versa? I have no idea. I was spending more time with Petticoat Boy, Roxy and even little Terry. Sometimes our film makeup artist, Lucy would hang around but Roxy seemed to find her annoying so that didn't happen too often. Spending less time alone might've made me a more pleasant proposition but I don't think that was it. Maybe I was just off my game. Maybe I'd grown up a bit. Grown up? I can hardly believe I said that. 'Growing up' is one of those phrases that don't have anything to do with actually 'growing'. It's either used as an insult that's supposed to make you wither and wish you could be more mature (as in, 'Why don't you just grow-up Morrison!'), or a patronising compliment (as in, 'Wow, look at you all grown-up!') Growing up is more to do with fitting-in to whatever place or situation you find yourself in. It's usually to do with rules and regulations and when you show them the finger, apparently you're 'not grown-up'. Being grown-up is what most people wish for because it tells everyone else you've arrived, conformed, or become better at something, or not so ugly, or in my case not being a constant pain in class.

And it was true about me being like a botfly on the school's arse. Even I could see I was more than a bit of a nuisance. Didn't need to be a rocket scientist to figure that one out. I've explained how I behaved with some teachers and other so-called figures of authority. As far as my earlier anecdotes about Hamm, Cottrell, Jacobs and Rosario I don't have any apology for, although since the camp I had well and truly left Ms Rosario alone and by the way her belly was bulging she didn't have too much longer to go at Riverside College—and to be fair, she had seemed to appreciate our little movie.

My favourite line of annoyance was to question what we had been asked to do, or to doubt something that was clearly true or accurate. Frankie, who was still my English teacher in Year 11, once asked me why I carried on like this. I could've given him any one of a number of answers, but I told him it exercised my mind compared to what we were usually confronted with in class. Bit tough on Frankie—after all it was him who put me onto John Morrison and thus my name. Some teachers kind of enjoyed my little riddling line of questions while others wanted to throttle me. I'm sure a few would've been able to leave me dead in the classroom and go home to their lovely families, eat dinner, play games with their kids, watch TV and fall into bed, satisfied they had rid the school and possibly the world from the curse of Morrison.

I had a Maths teacher, Bernie Kriaris, who was bald as a billiard ball but insisted on the dreaded comb-over. He was renowned for having Year Seven kids walking behind him snipping at his hair with imaginary scissors. But having a shot at him over that was as pathetic as his comb-over. I preferred to discuss with him in class some of the basic tenets of Mathematics. He was mad keen on Algebra, Geometry, Trigonometry—said it was the basis of humanity. Mmmm. Anyway after some online sleuthing at night when I couldn't sleep, in the middle of some maths work I raised my hand. Bernie finally noticed my hand waving in the air like I had a lighter at a music festival.

"Yes," asked Bernie. "I'll be with you in a minute, Morrison."

"But Sir, I don't think this can wait."

"Why not?" he asked, doing his best to appear calm in the face of some Morrison nonsense.

"Well, Sir—Bernie—I don't see how I can go on with doing Maths if some of the things I've held to be true for years just aren't true." Now I had the whole class on board and Bernie knew it. Not that I was the popular kid in class, far from it. It was more that it sounded interesting.

"It's all about two plus two," I said.

"Are you talking literally or figuratively, Morrison?" Now, even though he had a comb-over and was dribbling mad about Maths, it was his curiosity that got him hooked. Every time I raised some doubt or question, even though he knew I was entertaining myself (and maybe the other kids in class who also told me to shut my mouth) he was a true teacher. Can't believe I just wrote that but after years of being stranded in one school or another you get an inkling of what that means. He loved his subject. He loved getting kids onto the Maths train. He even loved the kids who never understood Pythagoras' theorem but for some kids when the penny dropped six months or a year later you'd think it was the best thing that had ever happened in the life of Bernie. Like happy happy happy. And if you became what they liked to call 'a disruptive influence' he never called in the Year Co-ordinator or the Vice Principal and he was one of the rare breed who never sent me to Mr Moore's office. Although maybe he should've. And there's one more thing about a true teacher like Bernie—they know their stuff so well they can explain it simply.

But all those nice words didn't stop me from my 2+2 escapade.

"Figuratively or literally, Sir? Mmmm... not sure. I think literally."

Bernie wandered up to my table, flicking a pen around in his fingers. He had a smile trembling at the corners of his mouth that looked like a smirk.

"Go on, Morrison," he murmured.

"Well I got the idea from a Russian writer called, Dostoevsky who reckoned that it was our choice whether we went along with the idea of two plus two equals four—like it's all logical but if we feel like it we can say nah I'm not going along with all that logic. If I want two plus two to equal five then I can be illogical if I want to."

At this stage I should tell you that I only came across what one of Dostoevsky's characters said when I googled it. Even though I quoted him I'd never read any of his books—but after finding that kind of weirdness I intended to read some. The main reason I quoted him was to unsettle my audience. If you tell people that sort of info, it impresses the hell out of them and they're just about ready for anything—as you're about to see.

"You know this is not a Philosophy class, don't you Morrison?"

"Yep, pretty sure I do, Bernie but let me tell you and you'll see it's all to do with Maths. Y'know how we have to round up or round down numbers when they've got a fraction to them, like 7.3 goes down to 7 or if it's 7.8 it goes up to 8?"

Bernie smiled, seemed even relaxed. The rest of the class had stopped working which I hardly realised because I had to keep my wits about me to get the explanation clear.

I went on. "Soooo—if you add 2.3 to 2.4 (both of which would normally be rounded down to 2), you get 4.7 which rounds to 5. Like magic you get 5 instead of 4!!

Bernie did this snorting laugh and even a few of the Maths nerds clapped. The rest of the class told me I was a dickhead, one threw a pen at me while others asked why didn't I spend more time looking at porn instead of dorky Maths tricks. I had hoped I'd annoy one of the nerds or at least Bernie by declaring that if I couldn't rely on such basic foundations for maths then how could I continue to learn. But the class went on as before and Bernie for months after looked quizzically at me every time he passed me in the hall.

Sometimes the best laid plans of mice and men come to nothing—or maybe to a place you never intended or imagined.

Like the Media assignment where we had to prepare, shoot and edit an interview. It could be with anyone—well known, infamous, famous, good hearted or nasty. We had to work in groups again, so it was clear to me, Roxy and Petticoat that we were the group. We were sent outside to discuss our ideas. We three sat at Roxy's favourite smoking lounge out the back of the school, looking down on the lazy ol' river ambling its way to the sea. It was the beginning of Spring, so we lay on the grass under a budding jacaranda tree. Petticoat started coming up with ideas straight away while Roxy blew smoke rings and I gazed through the branches and lime green shoots. I could daydream my life away if I wished. Even as a five year old, this is what I did. If I was alone, if I was hungry, if I was left, if I was with other little kids who knew I didn't quite fit the jigsaw puzzle, waiting outside Mr Moore's office, collecting trolleys at the Super—it was the Morrison Planet of Imagination that kept me on this planet. No wonder I liked writing.

"Hey, you guys, I know this bloke who's been cross-dressing for most of his life. Reckons the most amazing people have been into it—Peter Brock, the racing driver, some wood chopping champion, even the late boss of the FBI, nasty J Edgar Hoover liked his leather and lace, although he hated queers."

"So he hated himself?" Roxy asked.

"Looks like it." Petticoat nudged me with his foot. "Wadda ya reckon?"

I dragged myself back. "Worth a try. Why don't you give the bloke a call? See if he's interested."

Petticoat wandered off to make a few calls. Rox looked at me. "You don't seem too interested, mate. How come?"

"Oh no, good idea. At least it'd stir things up a bit. I dunno. Doesn't really grab me." I went back to my study of the sky through the leaves. Marcus returned with a frown. "The bloke's gone to live in Tasmania. Apparently he's got a boyfriend down there who wants to get married. Maybe we should go down there and film the wedding and do the interview with the happy couple."

Well obviously that wasn't going to happen. Roxy was staring at me, a tiny grin at the corner of her mouth. "You sure you haven't any ideas, Morrison? C'mon, you never seem to run out of them." She took a heavy drag right down to her lungs that were just waiting for emphysema to visit. She moved right up close to me and blew the smoke straight into my face.

"What the…! What'd you do that for?!" I spluttered. "Jesus Roxy."

Petticoat had no idea what was going on but by the mischievous look on Roxy's face she knew exactly what she was doing. "Come on Morrison! Stop being so bloody coy and mysterious. Out with it. I know exactly what's going on in those weird little grey cells of yours."

I tried to ignore her provoking and bluster my way out of it. "Oh right, you're not only the director, now you can read minds."

"As a matter of fact, sometimes I can, especially when they're as see-through as yours at the moment." Roxy got up and sat on me. "Get off you bloody clairvoyant! Weirdo!"

"Takes one to know one, Morrison. Only getting off when you spill your guts."

Petticoat looked on as though there was something going on that he couldn't grab. Roxy remained squeezing the wind out of me. "Get off Rox. I'm going to fart."

"Wouldn't be the first time I've smelt them." She tossed her head back and laughed. In that split second I saw how good-looking she was, a green-eyed girl with mystery and devil in her face, matching green streaks in black tousled hair. I grabbed hold of her and rolled her off. "OK. OK. OK," I laughed.

"You two finished with your flirtations," Marcus jibed.

Me and Roxy looked at each other like startled rabbits. Roxy went the colour of a summer tomato, exclaiming, "What, me and Morrison?! You gotta be kidding. It'd be like getting off with my brother." She quickly searched for another ciggie in her packet.

Petticoat Boy smiled quietly to himself and said, "Yeah, yeah, sure. Anyway, what's Morrison hiding from us? Is he going to tell us or will you?" Roxy had moved away from me, allowing her discomfort to be packed up and hidden away.

"I know I can trust you guys so if you think I've gone a bit wacko (Grandma's favourite word for mental instability) or become obsessed, say it and we'll move on."

Petticoat lay back on the warm grass, put his hand to his forehead and said, "Oh right. I get it now. Of course." He paused. "He'll do it, I presume?"

"Sure to," Roxy picked at the grass and with a sideways look at me she giggled, "Especially if his new BFF asks him."

The next day in English I asked Frankie if I could go and organise something for the Media interview.

"Can't be done another time I suppose," he said quietly to me.

I glanced furtively around me. The rest of the class were getting on with their own short stories. "I'd rather not say, Frankie and anyway you know I'll do this work—I mean, I got a few stories at home I've been working on."

Frankie beamed. "Uh oh," I thought. Give a good teacher, a true teacher as I've called them, one tiny morsel of optimism, a hint you've pursued some school thingo outside the boundaries of their subject and it's enough for them to tell their teacher mates, tell their families, and skip down the hallway—although Frankie skipping was a sight to make me shudder and once I'd shuddered I couldn't help seeing him in a purple tutu, arms gracefully shaped above his head, pirouetting his jiggling body through the crowd of lunchtime kids.

"Off you go then, Morrison." Frankie's reply brought me back from his ballerina performance and to the job at hand.

Of course I didn't want to go see Mr Moore during any of our breaks. Our sort-of knowing each other had already been gossiped about but my reputation of sometimes going off like a cracker at least spared me the crap of hearing it. As I walked down the circular stairs I realised I'd never seen Mr Moore via any of the normal, more acceptable channels. I'd thought of getting chucked out of class but as I said, that had dropped off somewhat. Then I was there, at the front counter where every visitor to the school had to present, usually to get their visitor card. This procedure was to ensure that everything was above board and that they weren't accidentally giving access to a wacko (thanks Grandma, again), a potential axe murderer (yes, I think they're wackos too), an overprotective parent (frankly I wouldn't have minded one of those in my early school days), a jilted boyfriend who was looking for the one who stole her from him, or maybe her as well, or, and I've seen this happen, some dickhead gang member taking the fight from the 7Eleven into the school—I've only had small trouble from those blokes but sometimes you've got to feel sorry for those kids. I mean what would it be like walking around knowing you've literally only got half a brain and what remains is a serious psychosis and a half-baked dream of fighting in the UFC.

Anyway there I was ringing the little bell to get attended to. I waited five minutes and rang the bell three times in that interval. Finally, the big sliding door opened and out came Vera. Vera was tall, curly frizzy hair, glasses on a pink plastic chain. Everybody knew Vera—kids, teachers, canteen people, gardeners, even Morrie the cleaner with the suspicious scar on his forehead and somehow they all knew they had to work overtime just to get her attention, much less get something that approximated a smile from her. Vera was the boss of the front office and there was no way an axe murderer was getting past her steely glaze. Once, when I was outside Mr Moore's office I overheard a teacher being quizzed by Vera over a request for some envelopes. It was Ms Gerrard, my Lit teacher who had to answer Vera's cross-examination.

"How many do you want?" Vera queried.

"Oh six would be fine but to save me coming to ask again could I have a packet for our office?"

I heard the slight tremble in Ms Gerrard's voice.

"A packet?!" Vera sounded like this was the end of civilisation. "Ms Gerrard, if I gave a packet to every teacher who asked, our supply would run out in a week. Do you want them for school purposes?"

I could feel the teacher's face burning and I was sitting around the corner.

"Well yes, what else would I use them for?"

At this stage I felt like yelling out, "Gees Vera, don't you know she needs them for her secret love letters to Mr Hamm." Then again, Vera probably knew about their little tryst and was possibly why she was giving her such a hard time.

"Well OK Ms Gerrard. Here's your six and please don't make a habit of it."

I don't know what it was about Vera. Did she pay for the envelopes out of her own pay? Did her bonus depend on how many envelopes she had left? Or did she have a bad life, little or no love and enjoyed making others uncomfortable at best or frightened at worst? Or maybe she just didn't know any difference and thought that everybody behaved in this way. There are people like that. Beats me.

Vera was genuinely surprised to see me. "Morrison. What are you doing here? In class time?" she rasped. "Who said you were allowed to leave your seat?"

I felt like giving her a volley of my best: "Ah that seat is really uncomfortable, could you afford a lounge chair out of your budget? Think I'm coming down with a cold, could you fossick up a heater for me? Actually, it's not all that cold but I am getting an icy blast from the front office. I have to go to the toilet, would you mind saving my seat for me? Vera—were you born with a pinched, miserable face or did you pick it off a lemon tree?"

Of course I wouldn't have fired that last shot. Not even me on a very bad day could have come out with that but it was seriously tempting. "I'm not on the seat Miss. Not today at any rate (at this point I gave her a wan, entreating smile). I was hoping to see Mr Moore. It's about a school matter." Check out that word 'matter'. Sounds official, nobody knows what it means, and it rings with phoney sophistication.

"Why on earth should Mr Moore stop what he's doing for you?"

"Well Miss, Frankie excused me from class to see him. And, as I said it's a school matter. Would you like to check with Frankie?"

Vera's confidence shimmied, cracked and then began to crumble. She sighed with exasperation. "Stay here and I'll see if Mr Moore's available." And off she went. Goal to Morrison.

Five minutes later and Vera returned. "He'll see you now." Wow was she pissed off. Vera must've felt as though her boss had just stabbed her in the back.

"Thank you so much, Vera," I smiled.

"That's 'Miss' to you, Morrison."

"My apologies, Miss Vera. I won't do it again." I beat a hasty retreat before she had time to explode.

I knocked on Mr Moore's door and an almost inaudible voice said, "Come in." He was seated at his little coffee table, staring aimlessly out the window. I waited for him to know I was in the room. Finally, "Ah Morrison. Good to see you. What brings you to my office via normal, respectable channels?" Mr Moore smiled to himself.

Once I got through all the Frankie-let-me stuff and the negotiations with Storm Trooper Vera I began to explain the Media assignment but cut it short when I realised Mr Moore was hardly paying any attention to me. A silence entered the room like a long grey cloud, fat with rain, which made me nervous and edgy but didn't seem to affect the old man. In fact I don't think at that moment he knew that I was there, nor did he know where he was. I decided to sit down and wait till he returned. He was grey in the face, greyer than usual. His navy blue cardigan was crumpled, like he'd slept in it and his wavy silver hair looked like a bird had nested in there.

Mr Moore turned to me as though I'd just entered the room. "So, Morrison. How did you get on with Vera? I heard part of the conversation." I said nothing. "Yes yes, I know she can be a touch daunting but she's very loyal to me. Keeps the idiotic and mundane from my door." More silence. I could hear the quiet chatter in the front office through his door. "And between you and me, she's one of the few who know about Jenny... oh yes, and by the way I've appreciated how you haven't shared that with the whole school."

I decided to dive in. "How is your wife, Mr Moore?" He looked down at the floor and rubbed his hands together.

"She's not got any better I can tell you that, Morrison. She wakes up several times a night. When I'm about to do some work or maybe watch a movie, out she comes asking me what I'm doing, or if I can make her a cup of tea. Then she wants to sit up with me and look at the movie which she doesn't understand or asks me the same question over and over, sometimes about a scene in the movie that has happened only a minute ago. Then all of a sudden she'll ask about our daughter, Michelle, as though she's still living with us. Sometimes Jenny goes outside and calls her in for tea... but I doubt if she can hear her up there on the Sunshine Coast. I tell you Morrison, it's a very difficult time."

What could I say to the guy? What could a seventeen year old possibly say to a man in his sixties going through the ravages of his wife losing her mind. "That's pretty awful Mr Moore. Awful..." What a weak response that was, was all I could think. The grey cloud had become darker, heavier.

"Yes that's one of the words I could use. When I'm alone I can use other words..." Mr Moore looked straight at me. "I'm sure you understand." He laughed and dipped into his pocket and offered me a mint. The mint was like a ritual between me and Mr Moore, like the first time I found myself in his office and briefly wondered if he was a secret paedophile. I felt a bit ashamed at that, the poor old bastard. Here he was being kind to a kid who, as Willy put it, had a few 'issues'.. and all I could wonder about was whether he was a vile, dirty old man. I took the mint and put it in my mouth.

"So what was it you wanted, Morrison? Must've been fairly urgent for you to get out of class to come and see me."

After what I'd heard in the last five minutes made me think the whole interview idea was stupid. Like we're going to do some mickey mouse assignment with a man who's going through something others would find unimaginable. I looked up at the cloud which was now touching our heads. Mr Moore raised his eyebrows enquiringly. "Unlike you to say nothing, son. Come on, spit it out!"

I took the deepest breath I could and began this mad stream of consciousness about after his work on our movie we thought interviewing him was a great idea and that seeing he was about to retire and that he'd been a teacher for so many years that he might have some really good things to say, and some advice thrown in. When I finished he offered me another mint. "But obviously our interview idea hasn't come at a good time, so I'm sorry for bothering you and we'll find someone else. No worries."

I got up to leave. The cloud remained but not so menacing. Mr Moore looked up at me. "Where are you going, Morrison? You just got here." I sat down like the obedient puppy I was when I first entered the Principal's office all those years ago in Year Eight. I waited, in a ball of confusion.

Mr Moore sucked on his mint. I watched him rolling it around in his mouth. "Tell you what, Morrison. Let me think about it. Clearly the interview will have to be done away from school—otherwise it will be embarrassing for both of us. I'll have to check with the woman who comes to help me with Jenny. Better tell Izzy and Stan what you're up to... ." He stood up and did his customary rubbing of his knee. "Damn knee!" he said. At the door he shook my hand. "I'll let you know in a couple of days." He closed the door, and I could still hear him cursing his knee as I walked away.

CHAPTER EIGHT

I was in my Literature class when a Year 7 kid turned up. Years 7 kids took it in turns to run messages around the school—a bit like a walking email. And they loved doing it except if they had an older brother or sister in the school who would give them a real hard time if they turned up in their class. Older siblings seemed to think they had the right to say almost anything about their younger brothers and sisters. And they did. As soon as the little kid entered the room off they'd go: "What are you doing out of class? Piss your pants again? You stopped crying yet? Should've seen him/her this morning, blubbering over his weeties because he/she'd forgotten to get their excursion form signed." I felt sorry for them as they endured this gauntlet of insults but said nothing. The notion of Morrison coming to the little kids' aid would be about as helpful as Mr Moore defending me in a staff meeting. But I did reflect on the absence of brothers and sisters in my life. Maybe I didn't understand what was really going on with these taunts—maybe it was some twisted way of showing affection. Or maybe not. The older ones seemed to be embarrassed by their younger kin which I didn't understand and still don't. There were times I'd wished I had one or two of my own, if for no other reason to have company or know that I had some direct blood connection that was OK. Then again I wouldn't wish my father and mother on another soul.

Ms Gerrard went to the door. The boy handed her a note. She read it, re-read it and said thank you to the kid. "Morrison, apparently you're wanted downstairs." I stood up to leave but asked a question I wished I hadn't.

"Who wants to see me Miss?"

"Mr Moore," she said with a confused smile. "At his office."

Everybody in the class stopped what they were doing and stared at me. "He must've got lonely for you, Morrison. Must want to see you back on that seat where you belong." It came from Chris, the guy whose face I mangled with the hot pie. Why he was doing Literature I couldn't fathom. Over the years I'd never seen him with a book in his hand nor say one thing about any book—in fact, in another time and another country he would've been more likely to be burning books than reading them. A few retorts formed in my head but thought it better to make my departure smooth and say nothing. The last thing I wanted was to give any hint of what was going on.

Mr Moore was waiting for me when I entered. He seemed pleased to see me.

"How much time do you think you'll need, Morrison? The carer will be at my place looking after my wife, but I don't fancy being away for too long."

"Might take all afternoon, Mr Moore." I got an attack of the guilts, so I said, "Look Mr Moore, it's OK if it's too hard. We can..."

He cut me off. "No, no it'll be alright. But I wondered if it would be suitable if you did it at my house? That way I'd be around for Jenny if things became difficult but you and... who else is doing it, did you say?"

I stood there dumbfounded. His house?! His home?! "Oh, ah... just me, Roxy, y'know, the director and Petticoat... Marcus. Terry won't be there. Just us. You mean we shoot the interview at your house?"

"Yes, yes, my house. Is that too strange for you? Principals and teachers live in houses too." Mr Moore sounded irritated.

"No, no it's fine. Sorry. Just didn't want to intrude... with all your troubles as well."

"Well, we'll see how it goes. But I can't do it this weekend, it will have to be Sunday week? How's that?"

"That's good. That's excellent." I sounded as though I was gushing. "Thanks Mr Moore. Thanks."

Mr Moore stood up and ushered me to his door. "Alright Morrison, alright. You make it sound like you're interviewing a footy champion, or a film star... oh but that's right, I am."

Time for me to laugh. "Thanks anyway. I'll get your address later. I have to drop in your list of questions to make sure there's nothing there you don't want us to ask... or a question you'd like to be asked."

I worked my shift at the Supermarket that evening. Roxy and I had our break at the same time, so we sat out the back discussing the interview. We could take any course we liked, the person's past life, present life, big moments, things they were proud of, things they were still embarrassed by. We opted for his past life, how come he came to be a Principal, and how he thought his life had turned out. Stan and Izzie had warned us to be open to other stuff that might emerge that we hadn't thought of. When I told Rox where our interview was taking place she became like an excited little kid. "Cool," she kept on saying, "Cool." I hadn't said anything too much so far about Jenny and her Alzheimer's and decided not to at that stage. Who knows, the embryonic director might think she could do the interview with Mrs Moore instead.

Mr Moore and the interview was tumbling around in my head when I arrived home from work. I came into the lounge room but no grandma. Thursday was her daily intake of any Nature show that was on, but she usually started with the News, moved onto the Marngrook Footy Show and then prayed (she was big on praying—silently thank god) that David Attenborough would grace her TV.

"Grandma!" I called.

Nothing.

"Grandma?"

Then a faint 'in here' that came from her bedroom. I rushed in. Grandma lay in bed, her face sickly and blotchy.

"Oh Morrison, I'm so glad you're home. Don't know what's wrong with me."

I sat on her bed and held her hand. "What's going on, Gran? You don't look too well. You should've rung me. I could've left work early. Andy's not too bad about stuff like that."

Grandma put her hand on mine. "Oh it's probably nothing, dear. Could you get something for me? I'm terribly thirsty—have been for days. And hungry as well, like really hungry."

I gave her hand a gentle squeeze. "I'll get something for you. Have you eaten at all?"

"Yes, that's what doesn't make sense. I've been eating like a horse. And I've drunk so much tea and water I feel like a balloon."

I went out into the kitchen. It was a compact kitchen which is a nice way of saying it was big enough for a stove, oven underneath, a fridge that grandma was proud of because it was modern and made its own ice blocks, a bench to prepare on and a laminex table for eating. Not enough room to swing a cat in, as Gran would say. I was crap at cooking even though I had fantasies of cooking up food that would attract women and possibly seduce them, my staple of pasta and a bought sauce wouldn't get them through the front gate. Anyway that's what I knocked up plus a cup of English Breakfast tea, Gran's chosen top beverage—and that's not to say she wouldn't have a sherry before dinner and possibly a few glasses of wine when her gentleman friend Walter came over to watch telly together. However I didn't think alcohol was the correct choice in this situation.

I took it all into Gran who looked slightly better than when I first arrived home.

"What would I do without you, Morrison?" She hardly ever used my new name, but she was very happy not to have to call me, 'Norman'. I sat with her while she devoured her food and almost gulped down her cup of tea.

"Wow, where did you get that appetite from?"

"Been like that for some days now. Don't know what's going on… it's probably nothing." She looked at me, her pale brown face with her lovely blue eyes all crinkled. Grandma's smile fell on me like I was wrapped in a warm blanket.

"Well it might be nothing, Grandma but we better get to your doctor tomorrow. I'll take a day off school."

"Oh no, we can't have you missing school, darling."

"It'll be fine. No worries. And school will be glad to have a day off from me." Grandma laughed quietly almost as though she knew what I meant. "And I could drive you. We'll take your car, put the L's on and everything will be fine." Grandma looked at me through squinted eyes. "Come on Gran, don't give me that look. You paid for my lessons. You know I can drive. You can't go on the bus and why pay for a taxi when you've got a chauffeur."

During the night I heard her get up to go to the toilet at least ten times. She didn't look like she was dying but she did look and act pretty sick. I lay there, awake most of the night, thinking, dreading what life would be without her.

The next day, I drove her little old Toyota to the quack's (as Gran constantly referred to the doctor), with her frequently clutching at the dashboard and jamming her feet into the floor. After the chat and blood tests were all done, the doc was certain it was her diabetes 2 getting out of control. She wasn't too happy about that but as I told her, at least it was something she could do something about. Like exercise, eat better food, no more fried food, and alcohol was OK as long as it was a couple of glasses a day. But grandma was not one to take advice easily and she nearly dropped dead when I suggested that she might join one of those classes I'd seen on the telly, where older women do exercises in the swimming pool. In fact that's exactly what she said to me, "Drop dead, Morrison. If you think I'm getting my fat old podgy body into a pool with a whole lot of other tubbies, you're more silly than I thought you were."

"Didn't know you thought I was silly, Grandma," was my reply. She didn't come back at me because at that moment she yelped, "Watch the tram!!" To which I replied, "What tram?!" just to get her going.

So the next few days I stayed home and looked after her, which is what I told the school when I called them. Vera who took the call, didn't believe a word I said nor that I had a nice note from the Doc which I'm sure Vera thought I'd penned myself.

After that hiccup, Gran seemed to return to normal and once more sat in her chair in the lounge and ate some food I cooked (sausages and frozen vegetables done in the microwave) and complained about the plates of fresh fruit I put in front of her. While she sort-of thanked me her main gushy compliments were reserved for Walter, her old gentleman friend who brought over food that he reckoned he cooked himself. Which was pretty cool when I think about it. He didn't appear to be doing it for any reward, if you know what I mean, which if I was doing it for a girl I'd certainly have a reward in the back of my mind... well OK, I admit, there'd be nothing else on my mind.

I had four days of being a nurse for my old grannie. All I had to do was supply her with food and a bit of a chat. Which left me with plenty of time . I loved movies but generally telly and pay-tv bored me to death. Then I remembered the short story or essay assignment Frankie had given us: 'Someone close'. Obviously, my mother or trail of step-fathers would not be my choice. Then again, maybe they could be, which would give me the chance of pouring bile and vomit onto the page in a kaleidoscopic fury. But who would read it? And I doubted whether it would do me any good either. A cough from my gran's bedroom was all I needed. I pulled out my laptop, sat down and wrote:

'Grandma'

I think his name was Kevin. He worked on building sites, rough hands so tough you thought he could hammer nails with them. His face was rough-hewn, like a table that had been hacked out of a fallen tree. He could have been forty or sixty, very, very few words with a voice like mixing concrete.

It was him who turned up at my grandmother's front door one Saturday morning. It was Winter as I remember it. Grandma peered from behind her snibbed wire door. "Yes?" she said.

"I'm Kevin. I'm a friend of Cheryl, your daughter."

"Oh, yes," Grandma said, opening her door and stepping outside. That's when she saw me, holding Kevin's hand, blinking up at her.

"Sorry about this but thought it would be best if I brought Norman here."

Grandma tilted her head, locked her gimlet eyes on Kevin and said, "Go on."

Kevin shuffled around on the doorstep and rubbed at his stubbled face. "Well your daughter isn't the best at the moment. Going through a bit of a bad trot."

Grandma made a sound that was meant to indicate a lot of things, none of them very nice. "Run out of booze and drugs has she?!"

Kevin wasn't used to being taken on face-to-face. "Well, um, think it's more than that, missus."

Grandma finally looked down at me. It was like two strangers sizing each other up. Which we were. The Winter's sun had come out and I squinted up at her. Then she smiled at me. I don't think I'd ever seen a smile like that. Maybe others had. Maybe it was a normal smile. To me I felt like I'd been picked up and held close to a beating heart.

Kevin went to say something, but Grandma saved him the trouble. "Little Norman needs a roof over his head. I get it. Well he'll get one here. He's my flesh and blood." She reached out and took my hand, drawing me to her side. "But you can tell my daughter that she's not welcome. Unless she's done something about her ruined life. I'm not having her coming and going. If little Normie is with me, then he's with me. No ifs or buts."

Kevin nodded. "I'll let her know." He turned to leave, probably happy to escape the looks and words of Grandma. Halfway to the front gate, he stopped and came back. He placed his huge hand on my head, smiled and said, "See you, Norman. Sorry this happened." Then, "You're a good kid. Wish it coulda been different."

Grandma and me watched as he drove away in his battered ute, the sun shining full bore on what was to be my new home. My grandmother kneeled down and hugged me. "Come on Norman. Let's see what we've got to eat. You look like you could do with a good feed." As we walked inside she murmured, "So they still call you Norman... pity we can't change that."

I don't know whether she remembers saying that, but she got her wish.

It must have been hard for Kevin to turn up with me and do that. I'd had a number of step-dads which, let's face it weren't much more than a drinking, smoking, pill-popping, sleeping partner for my mother. But I remember Kevin as being a bit different. He was a big drinker and occasionally would fall off the edge, scaring the hell out of me and anybody else who happened to be in some house at some time. For the short period he was in my life I remember him showing me how to kick a footy and made me a bow and arrow from some wild, out of control bamboo growing in the backyard. I even remember my mother telling him off for spending time with me: "Come inside Kevin. The kid'll be alright. Come on mate. We got some serious shit in here for you. You just play by yourself, Norman! Mum and Kevin have to do some stuff."

Play by myself? I could do that. No doubt about it. I was really skilled at being on my own. Which is where my imagination, daydreams, really began. From a very young age I observed everything. There was nothing I didn't notice. I remember sitting in a parked car on Sydney Rd, in Brunswick watching hundreds of people walking by and to my amazement I realised that everybody had different faces, hundreds, then thousands of different faces. My imagination and the scenarios I laid out in my head was going to be the thing that kept me going, kept me going until I was presented to my grandmother one wintery Saturday morning. I think I was about six or seven years old.

I don't think Gran expected me to stick around but I did. It wasn't as if she thought I'd run away. It was more that she expected my mother to turn up demanding Grandma return me to her and her life. But if I'd had a say in it I don't think my choice would've been too difficult. There was my mother, with eyes and face like they'd had their say in what she'd put them through. Her face weathered and leathery, wrinkles and creases like a horse had pulled a plough across an unfertile field. Her life one deadweight after another—jobless (she had no desire for one at any rate), dole (spent on food, rent or medicine? Who are you kidding), friends (with friends like hers…), one battered, peeling, crumbling, broken down, freezing/boiling hot, house after another where we never stayed too long, and… and… and that's about it. That's all she wrote, as the song goes.

Why she was like this it was hard for a little kid to know, and let's face it, difficult for me to know at the age of seventeen. I don't think Grandma had much of a clue either but what she did know was how to look after me. I'd think of my mother now and then, but those gloomy thoughts would always be replaced by Grandma. She wasn't (and still isn't) much of a cook but she taught me how to make packet cakes, and heat spaghetti and baked beans out of a can—oh yes, and to make a cup of tea, which I realised was essential for Grandma's engine to keep on working. She enrolled me at a Primary School where I was treated kindly by the teachers, where at lunchtime I actually had a sandwich, biscuit and fruit in a lunch box and once a week I had money for a pie, a drink and a huge, pink iced coffee scroll. I still didn't know how to talk to other kids, but I could kick a footy pretty well but didn't know who to barrack for or even how you got to choose. Most of the others went for the team their dad, mum, cousin, Grandpa went for. I asked Grandma who she went for. 'Doggies' she almost yelled which meant that was to be my team.

At night in those early years Grandma read to me every night. You'd expect me to have missed out on that skill but strangely it was the one thing I could do. I think my mother may have read to me at some stage, but it doesn't remain as a memory. Memory is a slippery little thing. Some of them you're sure of but later that certainty starts to wobble. Other memories come bursting onto the scene and you wonder where they've been hiding. While others start from a speck and grow so quickly and intricately you're not sure which bits are true, and which are simply untrue. So my memory tells me that I think I kind of taught myself to read. My mother understood from early on that books seemed to shut me up so she and her boyfriends would now and then get me a book from the supermarket or from a second-hand shop. They were either simple little Golden books or worn and torn used ones from St Vinnies. Didn't matter, I could lose myself in them and see how others lived. I could have one fantasy after another which led me down some crazy paths. Like I began to believe that inanimate objects like shoes, toothbrushes and cutlery could communicate with me and each other. Their language was easy to understand and soon they were like my best friends. I wondered why my mother and her friends couldn't speak their language and why they couldn't be more like them. In the early days with Grandma, she heard me chatting to my pillow one night and asked me what I was doing. "I don't know, Grandma," which was good enough for her.

When she saw that I could read almost anything, she took me to the library, got me my very own card and from then on each week she and I would trot down to the library and make our selections. I would go for any book that got me in the first page—it could be about princes, gangs, frogs, naughty kids, good kids, other lands, made-up lands, while Grandma always went to the same section of the library where there were books with ladies and men kissing each other, angry, sad, laughing, but always with romance in the air. She'd lost her husband a long time ago, died from industrial poisoning, so I guess she had to get her dose of romance from somewhere.

Over the next number of years my grandmother took me to the footy where her passion for 'her' Doggies was embarrassing but the hot jam doughnuts and hot dogs easily made up for that. Some years later she suggested I go and watch the local team from Ballantyne which is when I started writing match reports for the local newspaper and where I made friends with a gun player called Johnny Carbone who didn't care about me being a bit different and who was later picked up in the Draft.

Sometimes Grandma would cart me along to one of her friend's places where they played cards, or to the supermarket, or the local fruit and veg market. She even attempted to organise birthday parties for me which never turned out quite what she wanted. Only a few kids came, most of whom went home early, no matter how many cakes, red snakes, green cordial and prizes she provided. Other kids, teachers, people at the footy or in the library—it was something I couldn't quite get the hang of. 'Relating to others', it was called, mainly on my school reports and if they gave marks for it I would've got a big fat 'F'.

I'll tell you who wouldn't get a FAIL. My grandmother. If it wasn't for her, and to be honest, Kevin as well, when Grandma and I came together on that sun-filled, wintery Saturday *morning I'd still be in a filthy bed, with an empty life and no idea of what was going to happen next. At least these days when I go to bed and wake up in the morning, I know there'll be one constant in my life.*

Morrison.
11B.

CHAPTER NINE

I returned to school the next week. Roxy had the list of questions ready for me to deliver to Mr Moore.

"Why didn't you give it to him?" I asked. We sat out the back with Petticoat Boy.

"Oh sure," she said, sucking on her cigarette as though her lungs were crying out for more. "Then I'd be known as Mr Moore's second best friend evaaah." As she said this she placed her hand on my face and gave me a little pat. Petticoat smiled at us as though he knew something we didn't and went back to listening to his music. Marcus was his own person. Not easily bossed around—Roxy had tried but failed—content to be his own boss. Me and Rox had no idea why he wore petticoats, usually over jeans but in Summer he wore them over shorts. He was no idiot. There'd be plenty of kids who'd try and yank off the petticoat to see if all he had on underneath were jocks. He might've been gay, he might've been bi, or he might've been hetero with a penchant for petticoats. Or... he might've liked pushing the envelope, shoving stereotypes in people's faces.

When I thought about it, Marcus was not all that different from me or Roxy for that matter. The way I behaved anywhere and in any situation (pick a card, any card) was as much in others' faces as Marcus' petticoats. And Roxy? Well she was happy as a little Vegemite (yes, Grandma again), with her colourful phantasmagorical collection of clothes, hair colour—although I could hardly talk. When I looked after Grandma, to pass the time I put a thick red streak through the middle of my hair—but Roxy did it with flair, even a touch of style. And she was very good looking, if the number of comments she got around the place and sometimes at work was anything to go by. One guy, Dale, who was in a few of my classes, kept on pestering her, asking for her mobile number, her email, her Instagram, her whatever until just to shut him up she told him she already had a boyfriend, which he presumed to be me. Leading to him blocking me on the stairs, banging into me at the lockers, calling me a poofta (oh how that burned me, just burned...) among other things and telling Chris, the guy whose face I shoved the pie into, that I'd written a story about him getting his face sizzled. So Chris started his own guerrilla warfare of spitballs, bumping, shoving and oh yes, calling me a poofta and asking loudly at the canteen when me and Petticoat Boy were going to 'come out'. Fair dinkum, if either of them had half a brain between them, it'd be lonely. I mean these guys were sixteen/seventeen and to think they were probably only ten years away from having their own kids which does make me think that when people say there should be a parenting licence, they have a point.

Roxy didn't want to take the heat off me, in fact she wanted these two Neanderthals to fully believe I was her boyfriend, her soul mate, her partner to be, her forever and ever—so what did she do, kissed me in the corridor at lunchtime. Not a peck, not a brush on the cheek. Oh no, not Roxy. A full blown, open mouth, her hands around my neck, enough tongue to make sure everybody knew it was halfway down my throat, enough noise to get the attention of others who hadn't been paying attention and no A-frame hug but a full body press, top to toe. When she finished the performance with a crowd whistling, clapping and demanding that 'we get a room', she whispered in my ear, "Keep smiling, don't let the others think it was just an act." I adopted a look that said, 'yeah sure, we do it all the time, what's the problem?' and sauntered off with Roxy heading out the back of school.

"Wow, what a scene Rox. Soooo believable! Although they'll still be pissed off with me, but I guess I can handle them. You shoulda warned me."

"Nah," she replied. "It wouldn't have worked. They would've seen it for what it was. What'd you think of my performance, eh? Might take up acting instead of shooting movies."

We laughed and hugged each other like good mates but the taste of her mouth still lingered. Perhaps Petticoat Boy did know stuff that we didn't.

After school I caught a bus and got off at a stop close to where Mr Moore lived. 76 Dudley St. It was easy to find. A large weatherboard house, a fence with peeling paint, a once-neat garden that needed tending, a cracked concrete path to the front door, a small porch and a front door with a stained glass picture of a kingfisher above it.

I remembered Mr Moore's comment about teachers being normal, with normal families, normal streets, living in normal houses. 'Normal' wasn't something I knew well nor overly trusted. The bell was a tiny porcelain button set into a brass surround. I drew a breath and pressed it. Faintly, I heard a tinkle from the back of the house. Like an ice-cream van when it's a street away from yours. Silence. Then: "I'll get it." A person walked along a hall to the front door. Not Mr Moore and certainly not his wife unless everything I'd read about Alzheimer's online was wrong. The door was opened by a Vietnamese woman of about fifty wearing clothes that looked like they belonged in a real estate office.

"Yes?" she said. Then she took another look at me and gave me a half smile. "I think you want Mr Moore?" she asked with a raised eyebrow. I nodded. "Mr Moore!!" she called. "Someone here for you."

In the shadows of the hallway, Mr Moore appeared behind her. "Yes Grace, who is it?"

"It's me, Mr Moore. Morrison."

"Oh Morrison. It's alright Grace. This is the young man I was telling you about. Morrison, this is Grace. She helps look after Mrs Moore. Come in Morrison. I was just having a cuppa. Come down to the kitchen and meet Jenny."

Now all this sounds completely normal doesn't it? Ring a doorbell. People answer it. Invited in. And so on. But I'm a kid (and a somewhat troublesome kid) from the school that the old bloke is in charge of. He's in his after-work clothes—a pair of grey trakkies, and slippers, and I'm being led into a kitchen to meet his wife who is in the depths and throes of a memory sickness called Alzheimer's. Before I had a chance to blurt out *it's-all-been-a-terrible-idea-and-I-don't-want-to-trouble-them-and-what-was-I-thinking-doing-an-interview-with-Mr Moore-in-his-own-home* I was in the kitchen looking at a small old lady who sat at the kitchen table in a pair of navy blue slacks, a bone coloured cardigan, lamb's wool slippers and a large serviette tied around her neck. She had this lovely smile, like I imagine someone saintly could bestow on the world's troubled and downtrodden. I've said that she was old, but she could've been fifty or eighty.

"Jenny, I'd like you to meet Morrison, a boy from my school."

I held out my hand which she softly took in her hand. "Hello, Jen-, ah Mrs Moore."

"Doesn't matter, son. She likes being called Jenny," Mr Moore smiled, picking up a piece of cake that had fallen from her mouth. Jenny kept smiling at me and didn't let go of my hand. This was awkward but didn't seem to faze Mr Moore, or Grace and certainly not Jenny.

"Better let go of his hand now, Jenny. He might need it to write with, eh Morrison," Mr Moore said with a soft laugh. "Would you like a soft drink, son?"

"Ah sure, thanks," I said as I slowly extricated my hand from Jenny's grip.

"Would you like a drink?" Jenny asked me. I smiled at Jenny, but my face said confusion.

"That's OK Jenny. We'll get him a drink." Grace, the carer moved around the kitchen, rinsing plates and cups in the sink. "I'll bring the washing in now, Bill, before I go. The interview is this Sunday, right?"

Mr Moore nodded. "Now Morrison we better have a look at these questions you're going to ask me. Better see if I've got answers to them... otherwise I'll have to make it up." For some reason Mr Moore found this to be hilarious. And for some reason so did Jenny who laughed along but clearly not aware of what she was laughing at.

When they both stopped laughing—Mr Moore first and then Jenny taking her cue from him—Jenny took my hand again and asked, "Would you like a drink?"

I'm never really lost for words, but this repetitive questioning flummoxed me. I smiled politely, held up my can of drink to show it to her, looked at Mr Moore for help but he just let it go. Then Jenny unleashed her smile again and this time I saw it not so much as saintly but something she did that she might have remembered from her past. She took another shaky sip from her cup of tea, a bit of cake which mainly landed in her lap, looked out the window where Grace was bringing in the washing. "Who's that Bill? Someone's in our backyard."

Mr Moore looked up from reading our questions, smiled patiently but tiredly and said, "That's Grace. You know, the woman who helps me look after you."

"Look after me? Look after me!? I don't need looking after." Jenny's smile had faded, replaced by a mixture of confusion and anger.

"No. No darling, you're right. You're doing fine. Grace just does a few little jobs here and there."

This seemed to pacify the old girl. She slopped a bit more tea and then asked Mr Moore, "Who is this young man? What's he doing here?"

Grace entered the kitchen with a basket full of dry clothes and broke the scene which Jenny had no memory of at any rate. She picked up something from the table. Mr Moore smiled with relief and then explained. "It's a snow dome, Morrison. You love the snow domes don't you, dear. You've got quite a collection." Jenny however didn't listen or pay any attention because her full concentration was on the snow dome which was a tableau of a number of little elves loading Santa's sleigh which became covered in snow every time Jenny shook it. Mr Moore took advantage of this lull and said, "Well Morrison, the questions are all manageable."

I shook myself to come back to the business of my visit. Mr Moore and Grace simply went on with whatever they were doing, while my mind was all over the shop, with drinks being offered to me every minute, people being forgotten, cake spilling onto her serviette, the same questions asked over and over and then out of the blue along comes Mr Snowdome. At the start I may have been a bit off centre just by being in The Principal's own home and meeting his wife but all that fell away when confronted by the reality of Alzheimer's. But the best was yet to come. As I went to leave, saying polite goodbyes and thank-yous, Mr Moore said rather loudly, "Our guest is leaving now Jenny. But he'll be back on Sunday." Mrs Moore kept looking at her snowdome but as I went to walk out she exclaimed. "Oh that's right, you're that friend of Michelle's. She didn't come home for tea last night so when you see her tell her to come straight home from school and no dilly-dallying." I had no response to give but Mr Moore came to the rescue. "I'm sure he will, dear. No worries about that, eh Morrison?"

"Oh no, I mean yeah, no worries at all," I babbled.

When we got to the front door, Mr Moore smiled—but man, was it a weary smile or what! I'd only been there twenty minutes and felt like I'd been run over by a truck.

"You handled the situation very well, Morrison. It's not easy, is it?"

I shook my head in agreement and in a bit of a daze I replied, "No, no not easy at all." But what I really thought was that 'not easy' didn't even go close. It was like escaping from a house fire and saying, 'whoa, that was a bit warm'.

Mr Moore shook my hand. "See you at school perhaps but definitely this Sunday. The questions were fine, but I presume it will be OK if I add a bit here and a bit there? How about we start at 1. Jenny will have finished her lunch and with a bit of luck she might have a nap, but she'll be alright. She quite likes sitting around and watching what's going on... even though she understands less and less these days..." Mr Moore looked out at the street. "To be honest, she understands very little."

I decided to walk all the way home. I'd stopped riding my bike at the start of the year because of the hoons on the road chucking water bottles or projecting huge globules of green spit at me. As well, I was 17 and felt as though I was somewhere between a bike and a car. I wandered home, not being able to get rid of the picture of Jenny, cake crumbs, spilt tea, serviettes as big as a tablecloth, her sunshine smile that quickly changed to storm clouds and back again. Usually I could entertain myself by running a sarcastic monologue in my head but my normal schtick didn't prevail. In fact it didn't even make it out of first gear.

After my Jenny experience I knew that I'd have to run it by Roxy and Petticoat before the interview. When I got home it was late and Grandma was preparing to go out to the movies. Her boyfriend, Walter was already there. I was not allowed to refer to Walter as her 'boyfriend'. Gran preferred 'special friend', or 'companion' and I probably preferred those terms as well. Once you start with 'boyfriend' it doesn't take too much imagination (of which I had copious amounts) to take it into realms I would prefer not to go.

I was late home, and my dinner was covered in tinfoil. I told them where I'd been, which was unusual for me but that shows how disturbed I was from my encounter. "Alzheimer's eh," said Grandma. Looking at Walter she said, "Now there's one thing you and I could well do without". She glanced at me then said, "Although I've heard a lot of jokes about Alzheimer's... like, 'what's the best thing about Alzheimer's?— You meet new people every day!'"

Walter cacked himself with Grandma being pleased with his response. Her dog, Einstein woofed in appreciation. I did nothing. Said nothing.

"Oh come on, Morrison, that doesn't tickle your funny bone?! Try this one: A man goes to his doctor for tests and the doctor says: Unfortunately, you've got Alzheimer's and cancer. And the man says, That's OK, it could be worse, I could have cancer." Grandma and Walter broke up laughing. Gran looked at me and said, "Come on, my boy. Unlike you not to enjoy a joke in bad taste."

My grandmother knew I had a well-developed sense of humour. Once I had come across jokes and puns, wordplay and stuff, I began making them up myself. But these jokes went too close to the bone of my adventures with Jenny and a smile was a long way off. After they left for their 'date', with Walter still chortling, I got on the phone to Roxy and began the conversation with the two jokes. Roxy, true to form broke up laughing, so I guessed they were funny, just not the right time and space for me. Which made me wonder about a lot of my humour, which was often at someone else's expense—and possibly not the recipient's right time and space. But did that mean I was going to stop, cease and desist? Not likely. Way too much fun.

Sunday was two days away. I'd already informed Petticoat and Roxy about Jenny but I knew my words weren't enough for them to get what I was explaining.

"So this old lady can't remember things?" Roxy queried. "So what. Sometimes I can't remember what day it is. And I'm hopeless with names. Anyway, who are you? Remind me again." Roxy's attempt at humour received a guffaw from

Petticoat but again, somehow the jokes about Jenny and her affliction couldn't raise a smile from me. Sounds like I was being a wet blanket but my head was still getting around my one and only experience with Alzheimer's.

"Guys, look, OK I get the jokes but just don't think this is gonna be easy. She might stay there and say nothing but then again she could ask the same question fifty times and meet you over and over again. As if it's the first time. So you've got to be cool. And the old guy... well, y'know... it's bloody amazing he's prepared to do this."

Petticoat and Rox glanced at each other, smiled and nodded. Yeah sure, these two friends of mine reckoned they knew it all. There was nothing else I could say to lay the groundwork. They'd find out. And in one way I was laughing to myself about what was before them. But who knows, Jenny could maybe sleep the afternoon away lost in dreams she'd never remember. Then again...

The Sunday of the interview came and me and Roxy and Petticoat went and had a Vietnamese soup in Ballantyne. I'd decided to say nothing more about Jenny, Alzheimer's and so on—you know how they say, 'words can't describe' and normally I hate the expression but in this case, it came very close to the truth. We decided that Roxy would do the filming and that I'd do the questions while Marcus would fiddle around with the lights and reflectors. When we got up from our meal and left the restaurant I looked at Marcus. There was something different to him, I couldn't put my finger on it... then it hit me.

"Marcus. You're not wearing a petticoat! What's going on?! You decided to join the ranks of the normal and boring, eh?"

Roxy stopped and shook her head. "Hey, yeah, Petticoat. Where's your Petticoat? I thought you'd have a special one for Sundays."

Marcus looked around him at the rows of little shops, flickering neon signs and the string of cars snailing their way along the main strip and then back at us. He shrugged. "Can't somebody have a change just for the hell of it?" he grinned. "Don't want to become too predictable."

Roxy grabbed his bag and began searching through his stuff. "What the hell are you doing, you little bitch?! Give it back," Marcus protested.

Roxy skipped away, smirking. "Oh come on Petticoat, you must have some sexy little number hidden in here." Petticoat grabbed his bag back and kept Roxy at bay with his arm up. Roxy gave up trying to retrieve it and lit up a smoke instead. Looking at Marcus whose composure was shot I suddenly realised why.

"You're not wearing it for Mr Moore's sake! Oh right. Not shoving it in his face. That's pretty kind of you, mate." Normally I would've given him stick for reneging on his petticoat stance but in this instance... well, cool is all I can say.

We trooped off to Mr Moore's house with Roxy saying, "Hey Petticoat Boy, you better not stop wearing them at school. The homophobes will think they've won."

I rang the tiny bell which tinkled again. Once more Grace answered the door and was taken aback with us and all our equipment. "Hello Morrison. Hello you two. I'm Grace. Mr Moore is just finishing helping Mrs Moore with her lunch. Come in, come in. I think Mr Moore thought it best if you do it in the lounge room. That way Jenny can sit and watch if she feels like it."

We bundled our way down the hall, trying not to scrape the furniture or knock paintings off the wall. As we put our stuff down, Grace pulled me aside, speaking softly. "I hope this goes well today, Morrison. We've had a bit of trouble with Jenny last night and this morning, so if things go badly we might have to do it another day."

"What happened?" I asked quietly. Roxy and Marcus were busy setting up the camera and lights.

"Well, without going into it, enough to say she became very agitated, even angry. It was so bad that Bill rang me and asked me if I could come over. She objected to her dinner last night and threw it on the floor. Then she started swearing, and Mrs Moore never, never swears. Mr Moore tried to calm her down, so she kicked him in his leg, you know, the one with the bad knee. She walked out of the kitchen, and we thought she'd gone to her bedroom but when Bill went to check she wasn't there. Then there was a screech of tyres outside, so we rushed out and there was Jenny standing in the middle of the road, crying, angry and all over the place. By the time we got her back inside, she'd kicked Mr Moore again and was whimpering saying she wanted to die, she wanted a truck to run over her. I gave her some medication and apparently this morning she woke up as though nothing had happened." Grace heaved a heavy sigh. "Her condition seems to be getting worse faster than we thought."

Mr Moore entered the room. He looked like he'd been in a war. His Sunday casual clothes were neatly pressed black corduroy pants and a dark green cardigan over a white shirt, but his face said it all. Ravaged. Dragged through the mud. The lines on his face much more deeply etched, like fresh furrows in an old field, his eyes a paler blue, like some of his life had left, gone away, no longer able to hang around. He had dark bags under his eyes which held too much gloom and despair.

He shook hands with Roxy and Marcus. After all he'd been through the night before and that morning he could still manage to be amusing.

"Well, Roxy, I presume you are still the director, and your role hasn't been usurped since we last worked together?"

She had the good grace to laugh and smile. She had a great smile, one that could get under your guard if you weren't wary. "Yes I am Mr Moore. And Marcus will look after the lighting..."

"Ah yes Marcus. Welcome to our home, such as it is." Mr Moore examined Marcus closely. "But I see you've changed your attire. I hope that wasn't done on my account."

Petticoat Boy went red as a red red rose, dropped one of the reflectors and mumbled a complete lie. "Oh no, Mr Moore. Don't mind a change now and then..."

Mr Moore smiled and asked Roxy what I would be doing. "He's doing the interview Sir, if that's OK with you. I know he can be very annoying, so we'll keep him in check." Mr Moore laughed so loudly as if he was making up for a lack of it over the last few weeks. Here was Roxy, Petticoat and Mr Moore all chortling, cackling and sniggering at my expense. I pushed out a smile to show that I could cope having the piss taken out of me but truthfully I was a bit miffed. All three of them, none of whom would have been together on a Sunday afternoon at the Principal's house except for me—and now I'd become the butt of their jokes.

Roxy asked where Mr Moore would like to sit for the interview while Marcus fastened the lights into place. "Mr Moore," I said. "We'll just begin with a few straightforward questions, but I might need to ask some follow-up questions to go a bit deeper. OK?"

He settled himself in a red velvet chair with his hands folded neatly in his lap. "One thing before we start," he said. "As you know, as Morrison has already told you, my wife has Alzheimer's... advanced Alzheimer's actually... and she's not too well at the moment so we might have to stop now and then if Mrs Moore needs me or if Grace needs my help."

At that very moment, as if on cue, Jenny wandered into the room, wearing a pink and green floral dress, smiling ever so sweetly, with Grace hovering behind her. Looking at that face you could hardly imagine the rage and anger that had beset her last night. She stood still, looking at all of us. Mr Moore got up, his knees cracking, and introduced Jenny to us. Roxy went to shake her hand. Jenny didn't reciprocate but continued to smile this heavenly smile. Marcus grinned and nodded his head. Then Jenny decided to sit down on what was obviously her favourite lounge chair. Mr Moore moved closer to her, patted her hand, and bent over to her. "Oh so you're going to watch, are you Jenny? That's good. We might be a little while, but these young people want to ask me some questions. After we might go out for coffee." With a look in Grace's direction, Mr Moore sat down again. Roxy looked at me enquiringly. That was my cue.

"Mr Moore. You are now Principal of Riverside College. You are close to retiring. How is education different to when you first began teaching?"

Mr Moore glanced nervously at his wife who still beamed at her husband and began. "I was a carpenter originally, but I soon thought of teaching when they were short of trade teachers. The pay wasn't as good as a chippy—that's what carpenters were called—but the idea of passing on knowledge attracted me."

"So you were a carpenter who became a teacher. Did teaching turn out to be what you expected?"

Mr Moore laughed. "Teaching never turns out to be what you expected. It changes year by year, week by week, day by day. That's what makes it interesting."

Jenny sat there for ten minutes and then dropped off to sleep. An audible sigh of 'thank god' went around the lounge room. The interview went bowling ahead as though we all knew we only had very little time. Fifteen minutes later we thought it might be better if the old guy had a short break. Grace brought Mr Moore a cup of tea and we three were able to chat quietly.

"Going alright?" I asked Marcus and Rox.

"Sure, fine but what the hell were you going on about the old girl?! She's fine, says nothing, goes to sleep. No probs."

Marcus nodded in agreement.

"Well I wouldn't be too cocky. We haven't finished yet. And last night she apparently went a bit nuts. Yelling and screaming, kicking Mr Moore etc etc."

"Maybe she wore herself out," Roxy fiddled around with the love of her life, the Blackmagic camera. "Anyway, let's keep going."

The next fifteen minutes went smoothly. Mr Moore covered everything, no question was too difficult. He'd come from a family of six, parents both died early, lived in and around Ballantyne all his life. Was a union shop steward when he was a chippie, married after a courtship of several years, along came the Vietnam War, his number didn't get pulled out, so he wasn't conscripted but he opposed the war at any rate, had a daughter, called Michelle who married and went to live at Caloundra. And had two kids who they don't see too often. After teaching for fifteen years he decided to go for Vice Principal jobs and then became a Principal at one school until he got the one at Ballantyne.

"Why did you want to be a Principal?" I interrupted.

For the first time the old bloke stopped and looked down at the floor. He swept away non-existent crumbs from his trousers. "Mmmm, now that's a good one... to be truthful, I guess I'd been in a number of schools where the Principal in my opinion was no good. Not enough interest in what was being taught, how it was taught... and no real interest in the kids, the students. That kind of Principal always had their own career in bright lights. So I wanted to become one that wouldn't be like that... yes that's it, that's why I chose it."

The camera kept whirring, lights still reflected, stillness rolled through the room.

And then Mrs Moore woke up. "Toileting!" she demanded. "Toileting!"

Grace and Mr Moore sprang into action. "Sorry folks. Have to stop the interview for a minute. Come on dear. Let's help you up." Jenny was guided out, leaving a damp patch on her chair. Roxy took the chance to duck out for a quick smoke. Me and Marcus went out for a breather.

"Holy crap," Rox exclaimed, blowing smoke into the air. "Reckon we'll be able to continue?"

"Oh sure," I said without really knowing. "Although Grace told me sometimes she asks to go to the toilet fifteen times in a row. Doesn't need to, just gets stuck in a rut. Or forgets she's gone already. Or wants attention."

"Holy crap," was all Roxy could say.

"Where else is the interview going?" Marcus flopped down on the dry front lawn.

My answer was interrupted by Grace to tell us that we could get going again.

Once again in the room, all had returned to whatever normal was until Jenny caught sight of Roxy.

"Michelle. Michelle. You're home. What on earth have you been doing? Are these young people your friends? You didn't tell me you were going out. Honestly, young girl, what are we going to do with you. Come over here and sit down and tell me how school's going."

Roxy stood stock still, staring at Jenny, then me and then Mr Moore and back again. Like a kangaroo in a spotlight. Jenny had been smiling but seeing Roxy not doing what she asked, her face became a thunder cloud. "Bill, tell Michelle to come over here to her mother."

Mr Moore shifted in his seat. "Michelle is our daughter... would you mind going along with it? Just for now." Roxy flicked some switches on the camera and moved over to Jenny and sat down on the end of the couch. Mrs Moore took her hand ever so softly and didn't say another word. Sat there, smiling contentedly with possibly no awareness of anybody else in the room. This went on for ten minutes.

Now I want to get you to focus on this scene. There's Mr Moore, a kindly, soon-to-retire Principal. There's Grace, a Vietnamese-Aussie carer of Alzheimer patients. There's

Marcus from a Greek family who normally wears petticoats who out of some sort of respect has ditched his usual attire. There's me, Morrison who in some lunatic fringe of his mind thought that interviewing an old Principal, who he's known in some strange way for five years, at the Principal's home where he cares for his wife who has galloping dementia called Alzheimer's—was a great idea!

And now, if you were filming this you would zoom in on an elderly lady, Jenny who tenderly holds the hand of a streetwise girl, Roxy who she believes is her daughter, Michelle, as a teenager. Close-up of Roxy/Michelle. Face of utter confusion, a whirl of smiling, grinning, beseeching fear who now places her hand on top of Jenny's, enclosing it in warmth.

This had produced a calming effect, not just on Jenny but all of us. Mr Moore gave a tired smile, one that he was more than happy to have. Like water in a parched land. Jenny was content to sit there holding Roxy's hands, where she was most likely back twenty years ago, living under the same roof as her beloved Bill and her daughter, Michelle. I looked for a sign from Grace or Mr Moore. After patiently getting some comfort from the scene before him, Mr Moore leant over the coffee table in front of Jenny and Roxy and picked up one of several snow domes. Selecting one with a scene of a log cabin, a couple of animals grazing and a small shrub, he slid it over to Jenny, with a smile.

"Would you like to show Michelle this one, dear?"

Jenny picked it up, her smile turned into serene acceptance. But by now I knew that could become anything. Mr Moore said, "Michelle has some work to do for school. She's asking me some questions." Jenny absent-mindedly let go of Roxy's hand and turned her attention to the snowdome, giving it a small shake now and then. Mr Moore gave us a nod, with Roxy gently returning to her one true love, flicked on the switches and I started again.

"Mr Moore, being a Principal must be hard work—getting new teachers on board, looking after budgets, talking to parents, hearing complaints about the school or about students..." Mr Moore, Roxy and Marcus laughed softly in unison while I allowed myself a smile. "What do you do to relieve all that tension? Hobbies? Interests?"

"I have a shed out the back where I do a bit of woodwork. Keep my hand in, make small tables, chairs sometimes—not very good but I give them away to friends and they seem to like them."

"Could we see them at some stage? We can have you speaking while we show what you've made. Anything else over the years?"

Mr Moore looked at his wife. "One thing Mrs Moore and I did for many years was go camping. We both loved cooking outside, sleeping in tents, washing in the river—did a spot of fishing when we were at our favourite place."

"Don't like camping much—idea of all that bush and animals and spiders, sleeping on the ground."

Mr Moore laughed. "Oh Morrison, you don't know what you're missing."

"Anyway, where was your favourite camping place?"

"Outside Myrtleford. On the banks of the Buffalo River." He closed his eyes.

"They took us there in Year Seven—must've got the idea from you. Ended badly though."

Mr Moore again swept imaginary crumbs and dust off his black cord trousers. "Oh yes I remember that camp..." He shook his head. "But it didn't stop us going back there several times. Great times at Buffalo River, eh Jenny?"

"Oh Buffalo River. Camping—so lovely." Mrs Moore sat up, eyes bright, smiling broadly at her husband. The rest of us were dumbfounded, except Mr Moore and Grace. Roxy swivelled the camera onto Jenny. "Yes, one time we caught six fish, trout weren't they Bill?"

"Yes they were, and we ate most of them that night and shared some with other campers." Mr Moore reached out and squeezed her hand. "Good times, darling."

By then the Buffalo River, trout, tents, campfires and a river gurgling by had left Mrs Moore who once again returned to her log cabin covered in snow.

We finished the interview knowing that Jenny's patience, or whatever it was, could dwindle at any moment. We packed up quickly, thanking Mr Moore and Grace (and Jenny). As we did so Jenny lent her head back and began to run through a list that hid somewhere in her brain:

"There is something I have to do, I can't get it done."

"I've got to do it now."

"Is everything shut up?"

"Put things in their place."

As Mr Moore showed us out, he said, "She goes through this list several times a day. Grace and I usually nod and tell Jenny that we will. Anyway, thanks for coming and... and... being so professional. You all showed great kindness to my wife. Especially you Roxy, thanks." He went to close the door but thought better of it, calling after us. "Aaah, I was thinking that it would be better if you didn't use any footage of Jenny. If she had all her faculties I don't think she'd like it. OK?"

"Mrs Moore is safe with us, Mr Moore. No worries. We'll scrub out anything she might've said or did." Then I had one thought. "Although as long as we show it to you first, your memories of going camping and Mrs Moore remembering too—it might be a nice, might be a good thing to keep in. Would that be OK?"

Mr Moore hung onto the door. "Yes... I think so. We'll see... it's one of the strangest things about Alzheimer's, you know. Forever, kind of locked in the present and then all of a sudden she'll come out with a clear distant memory." He paused. "I'll go in now. See you," and the old Principal returned to his wife who on some days wasn't sure who he was.

We walked back to a bus stop with Petticoat saying his goodbyes.

"That was far out, like faaaaar out," exclaimed Roxy lighting up a ciggie.

I blew exhaustion into the air. "Jesus, imagine dealing with that every day, all day. For once in my life I got nothing to say."

She gave me a small hug. "Well that's something good that came out of this arvo."

"Oh so very funny... MICHELLE." After that one she punched me in the arm. "So Roxy my friend, you wanna come home to my joint. Stay the night. Grandma does some kind of roast every Sunday night. It's about the only thing she cooks well, otherwise I wouldn't bother inviting you."

That night Grandma, Walter, Roxy and me sat around the table where Einstein took a liking to Roxy and lay down under the table at her feet. We sat around the laminex table in the kitchen eating roast lamb, potatoes, pumpkin, peas, gravy, mint sauce—wow, just like a 'real' family. Grandma wanted us all to hold hands while she said grace. Gran had been attending the Christian Spiritualist church after sampling a number of others which offered activities like speaking in tongues, mass confessions for supposed sins, money donations, trips to Africa to dig wells and so on. None of them had got her until she came across this 'spiritualist' church to which she'd taken (dragged might be more accurate) Walter along who was not enthusiastic but went with Grandma to keep her company.

"Well Roxy, lovely to have you here. Tell me, do you believe in God?" Nothing like jumping in the deep end, eh Grandma. Roxy looked at me, put another forkful of food into her mouth, ate thoughtfully for a minute and then said, in true Roxy fashion, "No, I don't. I'm an atheist."

Walter allowed himself a small smile while Grandma put down her knife and fork and said, "Never mind dear, you'll see the light one day. It took me some years to see the light but at last the Lord has switched that light bulb on. Even Walter, here, has had some flickerings, haven't you Walter?"

"Not sure if it's flickerings but I'm interested. Possibly due to my age—getting closer to meeting the Maker so maybe just a bit of insurance," Walter replied, looking at Grandma.

Roxy and I laughed out loud. "Are you an atheist too Morrison?" the old guy asked.

"Probably more of an agnostic, Walter. You know, a dollar each way."

Roxy popped the last extra potato into her mouth (that girl could certainly eat). "Agnostics are people who haven't got the balls to be atheist, Morrison!"

My Grandma and probably Walter too were what you call open-minded but Roxy's straight-out 'balls' comment was met with a silence that spread from Grandma's plate, over the salt and pepper, around the remaining roast lamb and stopped in front of Roxy, who blushed, and fiddled around with her food, until she said, "Whoops. Sorry about that."

"It's OK dear," Grandma murmured, "I'm sure God doesn't worry too much about small sins, it's the big ones he's after."

From there we moved onto dessert (tinned peaches and cream), a bit of talk about the footy, and then Grandma asked about our interview. I said very little but Roxy, in order to really cement her name in the good books, described our afternoon in the land of Alzheimer's.

"Did you know, Roxanne, that our Morrison here hardly told us anything about Mr Moore and the interview. And what's more," Grandma continued, grinning straight at me, "he apparently doesn't have a sense of humour when it comes to Alzheimer jokes."

"Oh yes," Roxy joined in, ensuring she became a big soft spot in my grandmother's heart, "he told me them. I almost pis..., ah, died laughing."

Walter folded his napkin, excused himself and said, "Humour doesn't have to be cruel. It's something that helps us get through." Which sounded as though Mr Moore had joined us at the table. "That reminds me, if you want to join the Alzheimer's protest march, you must learn the chant:

What do we want?

I don't know!

When do we want it?

Want what?"

Roxy and Gran almost choked on their last mouthfuls. Walter smiled at me in what I presumed was a grandfatherly way. Me? I managed a smile, but the joke couldn't break through Mrs Moore's repetition:

"There is something I have to do, I can't get it done."

"I've got to do it now."

"Is everything shut up?"

"Put things in their place."

And a picture of Mr Moore and Jenny frying trout in a pan, camping next to the Buffalo River.

Chapter Ten

As I said earlier, the year I was 17 was a time that things changed. One change after another. One thing after another. 'Things' is a nice euphemism for not quite being able to put a finger on it. I could give a simple answer to 'what things?' like Mr Moore, Jenny, Alzheimer's, Grandma, Grandma's diabetes, my life as a little fella, Roxy, Petticoat Boy, Terry, our movie, the interview, my behaviour, sitting outside Mr Moore's office—but all the time this stuff was happening there must have been underlying currents beneath all those 'things'. Undercurrents, gentle then savage, flowing with me then against me. Pushing me along then dragging me under in a swirl of drowned branches and grasping weed. I may not be able to pinpoint what led to what, but this story allows for some kind of truth, some fathoming, to slip out between the lines.

One of those 'things' occurred when Grandma got home from her new church. It was earlier than usual because she enjoyed staying back after their service, having a cuppa and chatting to her new 'Spiritualist' friends. It was one in the afternoon, I'd just gotten out of bed, and I was organising some toast and coffee. I heard her come in the front door, but Walter wasn't with her. "Must've given God the slip," I thought. "Maybe gone to check why his 'light bulb' isn't working as well as Grandma's." I was on a roll with this train of thought when I heard Grandma go into her room, put her things down, but not emerge. I waited. Still no Grandma. I walked up to her room. She was lying on her bed with her shoes kicked off, her hand resting—no—not resting—holding her forehead. Next to her was her mobile phone.

"Grandma?" I asked quietly. "You OK? Is it the diabetes again?"

She took her hand away and immediately looked out the window, but I knew she was crying.

"No, not that, my darling boy. Wish it was. I don't want to tell you this, but I got a phone call as I left the church..." She fell into silence.

"And?" I said.

Grandma sat up and heaved a sigh. "And? Well it was Kevin, that man who brought you to Grannie's house all those years ago. He told me that your mother... my daughter... wasn't too well. Much worse than other times, he said. He reckoned that it didn't look good, that her liver and kidneys were packing up. She's in and out of hospital but discharged herself and arrived on Kevin's doorstep but he'll have to put her back in because she's so sick. Told me the name of the hospital if I wanted to see her..." It was too much for the old girl and she burst into uncontrollable sobbing and her body shook all over. My Grandma is probably the only person I can really give big hugs to, so it came in handy. I went over to her, wrapped my arms around her ample body and held her close, smelling her favourite apple shampoo in her grey hair. She resisted me at first but then allowed herself to be looked after.

"Would you like me to ask Walter to come over?"

Grandma could only shake her head. "Oh, how did it all come to this, Morrison? She was a lovely little girl, so happy, so interested in everything. And now... I'm so sorry Morrison. I wish I could've done a better job raising her. I think when your grandfather died it had a very bad effect on her but before I knew it she'd left home, moved up north with some people she'd just met. From then on, hardly heard from her and when I did it was asking for a loan, or telling me of some trouble she was in. I don't think she came back more than twice in all those years. Then she rang and told me she'd had a baby—you. She brought you to see me a few times over the years, but it upset me so much because I could see she wasn't looking after you properly." Grandma burst into tears, her whole body trembling like a tree in a storm." And I couldn't keep my mouth shut so when you were only three she said she wasn't coming back..." she blubbered. I was hearing a lot of stuff I'd only vaguely heard of in the past and it was having an effect on me like somebody had thrust their hand down my throat, reached deep into my stomach, grabbed a handful of intestines and twisted.

As much as I would've liked to expunge the rush of thoughts and memories flooding my mind I couldn't. That's the problem with not wanting to think about things—you can try and file them away in the filing cabinet of your brain, you can confront them and try and untangle or destroy them, or you can bury them deep in the cold hard ground. Filing cabinet method never worked for me—too precise, and hard edged and seems practical but the different folders keep spilling their contents into each other's defined territories. Confrontation was a path that some teachers, counsellors and social workers had encouraged me to follow, although they didn't see it as confrontation. They saw it as 'exploring' and 'working through' the cesspool of memories clogged in my young brain. Trouble with that is those doing the encouraging don't have to cope with the enormous amount of sewage that I knew would cascade forth if allowed to seep out. The 'explorers' would have gone home, clean and smelling pretty while I would've been left covered in excrement with no idea of how to clean myself up.

My preference, which shouldn't surprise you by now was the third option. Bury it all. Whenever I accidentally thought of my early young life, filled with only snatches of memory of which I had no idea concerning their reliability, it brought waves of nausea and anger. When I first arrived to live with Grandma I apparently used to wake up confused with nightmares and dreams and would burst into fits of young rage that seemed to come from nowhere. But Granny was no fool—she knew where it all came from. Wise Grandma or not, all she could do was console me and I nor her could ever get me talking about what made me like this. Yes sir, it was all buried deep down in the cold hard-hearted ground. I hadn't dug the grave and tamped the dirt down as a conscious act—that's simply the way it happened.

I have no memories of being belted, slapped or being sexually abused. As far as I know that never happened—more a general sense of, not just *feeling* but *being* left alone and lonely for such a long time. Neglect in all aspects was a way of life. Food, shelter, play, sleep, love, sharing, compassion—all of them left out in the rain like a favourite toy.

So bury it all! That's what I did all that Sunday. I thought of seeing Roxy but ended up walking the streets and finding myself at Buckland's Jetty. My favourite spot in the world. It was a Spring day with the weather not sure whether it wanted to be sunny with lilting cool breezes, sunny with heat that packed a punch, or grey clouds with a biting wind—weather which matched my mood. I went there in the afternoon and sat on the edge of the splintered jetty staring at St Kilda across the Bay with my idea of swimming from Buckland's to the other side. It was a constant notion of mine that could be interpreted as a death wish, a suicide waiting to happen, or as a fantasy I indulged in. That day it wasn't a death wish. Not a fantasy either. Nor was it suicide. Strange to say that avenue of despair never took hold of me. However I was having difficulty in burying the thoughts and emotions that whirlpooled around in my head. Buckland's Jetty normally fixed me up. But not on that day. Nor that night. And not when I caught the bus to Riverside College the next morning, for what was to be an eventful day.

Aaah good old school. I may not have really appreciated it, but it was a strange constant in my life. At least I'd been to the same one for a number of years. There we all were, baaaa-ing our way to home groups, telling lies about how fabulous our weekend was, exaggerating our different joys and angers, sly smiles to the hotties, blank faces to those we didn't like, a courteous nod to teachers we got on with. I, on the other hand, went out of my way to only give this nod to all the Hamms, Cottrells and Jacobs in the world. If there's anything that drives those teachers nuts who you can't stand is to greet them as if they're your best buddies. And they have no idea how to react. Poker face, scowl, sneer, purple arteries. I once witnessed Cottrell almost fall flat on her face tripping over a bag when confronted with a witheringly beautiful smile from yours truly.

This Monday was no different to all the others. Except—I had a head ready to explode. Only—I wasn't really aware of this which meant I was headed for real trouble. Feeling irritable doesn't really go close. Maybe an ants nest in my brain goes closer.

By lunchtime I'd managed to get through the rest of my classes with no fuss or bother. I'd done little work, but the rest of my teachers did nothing to disturb the dark brooding Morrison—which is clever teaching when I think about it. I didn't get lunch but got myself outside to our favourite spot where, thank god, I found Roxy. I sat down beside her, right next to her. Roxy took my hand and placed it on her lap. She knew me well.

"Don't want to talk about whatever is ailing you, sir?"

I managed a grin and shook my head. We sat there, no words, gazing at the river. The midday sun sparkled on the water, a million cut diamonds on its surface. For a minute I thought nature had got me out of the cesspool I'd been swimming in since Grandma arrived home from church the day before. The warmth of the sun, freshly mown green grass, new shoots on the trees, a tiny zephyr off the river—better than all the psychologists in the world, salivating over my train-wreck of an early life. But like Xmas when you're a kid, the good stuff doesn't last. Terry arrived, out of breath, his mousey face even paler.

"Morrison! Morrison! You gotta come! It's Petticoat—shit's hit the fan. C'mon mate, you gotta come."

"Hey Terry. Slow down, kid," Roxy tried to placate little Terry. "What's so bloody important? The place on fire?"

Terry started pulling on my arm. "Come on Morrison. They got Petticoat! Heaps of kids yelling and stuff. You gotta help him. It's that kid Chris—he's pushing him around. Trying to get his petticoat off. Top of the stairs."

I had been seduced by the sun, grass and river but the word 'Chris' broke the spell. Suddenly I was filled with all the gunk and vitriol again, what I'd arrived at school with that morning. I stood up and ran in one motion with Roxy and Terry charging after me. I ran without feeling. I ran without a human form. I was anger, energy and fury rolled into one. I know I must've been boiling hot, incandescent, but ice, thick blue ice coursed through my veins. I hit the bottom of the circular stairs, tossing kids aside like pieces of paper. I saw kids with their mouths opening but I heard nothing. I took the steps three at a time. In the middle of the crowd, kids all yelling about something. I finally saw Chris and Petticoat Boy, my friend Marcus who wouldn't hurt a fly, in a weird tangle of bodies. Chris had him in a headlock with one hand and with the other he was grabbing at Marcus' petticoat—his pink petticoat—trying to rip it off. Marcus was putting up good resistance, but he was up against a street fighter. One of those kids who reckon they've only had a good Saturday night if some kind of a brawl was involved. But I'm making this sound as though I was in some sort of rational state. There were a hundred kids, all genders, all races, all ages, all sizes. And there was Chris, a thorn in my side for years, always ready to make someone's life miserable. Petticoat saw me coming at them, shoving the spectators out of the way. He yelled, "It's OK mate. It's OK. I'm OK."

I launched myself at Chris, saying, "Don't care if you're OK, mate. I'm finishing this prick now!!"

I grabbed Chris the tormentor by his collar, ripping it in the process. He stopped for a minute and then seized Marcus' petticoat, tearing at it like it was a prize—a trophy for the bully boy cowards and the homophobes of the world. Then everything went into hyper drive and time and sense seemed no more. I lowered my head and drove Chris into the wall. I got fistfuls of his shirt and twisted them into tight balls of hatred. I had no idea where Petticoat was. And Chris didn't seem familiar. In all the flailing and yelling and pleading all I saw was my little bedrooms, overgrown yards, old cars, inside hot cars with torn seats, lying in bed with no sound coming from the rest of the house, fights, big fists crunching into cheeks, eyes, bloodied backs of heads, old raggedy kids books, a half-eaten sausage roll on the floor, shouting, tattered sheets, my Spiderman doona folded and put in another boot going to stay at another place where it was always going to be better—'you'll see'—and with a bit of luck into another kinder, or was it First Grade with no friends and who could blame them, and in all that time there was the ghostly figure of my mother, scummy dresses, tight jeans, stumbling, stupid sickly smiles sitting in a backyard filled with old trucks and cars, sitting in a shabby, tattered canvas sunlounge, morphing into a very sick woman lying in a hospital bed, machines blinking, tubes dribbling and sucking—which brought me back for a millisecond where I realised Chris and I were struggling at the top of the stairs and the whooping and cheering and encouraging had been replaced with the terror of silence but then the same movie returned with gusto and there was no human, no animal, no universal force that could or would stop me. I stared at my opponent, he could've been anybody, and slammed him against the metal rails, hard enough for his spine to take the brunt, I think I heard a muffled scream but who cares. I twisted him around so I could grab his belt from behind, swung him, then threw him down the stairs. I hurtled after him as he thumped and banged his way down, coming to a jolting end at the bottom where I jumped on him again and started laying into his face with my fists and every delivery was accompanied by pictures of my little childhood, my useless mother, my even more useless father until hands gripped me, pulled me backwards, off Chris and onto the floor where big hands seemed to hold me there. I struggled but I had nothing left in the tank and so lay there with my chest heaving, my body twisted, my breath coming in short, sharp grabs. I didn't get up. I couldn't get up. The hands that had restrained me were gone but I felt another pair of hands resting on my chest. Whoever it was couldn't stop saying, "Jesus. Christ. Jesus Morrison!" As my breathing returned, I looked up. Still heaps of kids milling around. Chris was rolling on the floor moaning and gasping. But there was no other sound. Like it was silent. More than silent. The complete absence of sound, as if everybody's heart had stopped beating. I looked up. There was Roxy, her hand stroking my battered face. "Jesus, Morrison," was all she could dredge up.

And then my eyes slid up and over to someone standing over me. "You done it this time, Morrison. Really done it. You coulda killed him. You're coming with me." As he hauled me to my unsteady feet, Hamm whispered to me, smiling, "And your *friend*, Mr Moore won't save you this time".

If I'd had one ounce of strength left in me, one scintilla of anger, I'd have belted him just to finish off a perfect day. Lucky I didn't but gees it would've felt good.

There I was. Back in my favourite spot. Where I wanted to be. Where I belonged. On my seat outside Mr Moore's office. Waiting. They put Chris in Hamm's office to make sure there was no follow-up blue. That wasn't going to happen. Chris was in no way, shape or form to go on with it. As for me, I was spent. I could sit on the seat but that was about all I could cope with.

Mr Moore emerged from his office, did a very quick glance at me and headed for Hamm's office. He had worry painted on his face. Not anger, no steam out of his ears— although as he quickly walked down the corridor he looked as if he had the burdens of the world carried on his back. For a second I felt bad. For no-one else. Just him.

They dealt with Chris first. Sensible idea. He was finally led out by Hamm who took him the long way, down the corridor, out into the canteen and then I glimpsed Chris and a teacher walking him out of school. Presumably driving him home. What his parents would say didn't bother me a scrap. I figured they'd seen their kid after Saturday nights, all bloodied and bruised. Although by the way he was walking he probably should've been taken to hospital. Then Mr Moore, closely followed by Hamm went into Mr Moore's office. Mr Moore took a quick look at me, while Hamm glowered, and I don't think it was my imagination, had a malicious grin on his fat face.

Meanwhile hushed groups of kids gathered at the end of the corridor, staring at me, still hoping for another exciting chapter in their boring lives. Willy and other teachers shooed them away, until Roxy appeared out of nowhere, slipping the gauntlet of officialdom. But she never said a word. Just squatted next to me on the floor, her hand on my leg, now and then checking me out. I returned her looks and saw that she was crying—quiet little tears rolling down her cheeks.

"It's alright, Rox. It'll be OK. They won't execute me or anything... except Hamm might suggest it."

But she couldn't raise a smile. And then through the throng at the end of the corridor, which kept growing, a teacher pushed his way through. It was Frankie. His chubby face, red as a turkey cock, was a picture of worry. For a second I thought he might cry as well. He stood there, looking at me, then Roxy, then back at the crowd of kids. Finally he said, "Jees Morrison. What the hell happened? I just heard. It's all over the school." He forced a smile. "And why wouldn't it be?!" And then, "How are you? Got any injuries?"

Now that dumbfounded me. There was Chris looking like he'd been in a car accident. There was me, the monster who'd caused it and whose fate was being decided in Mr Moore's office. And Frankie's asking how I am.

"Not too bad, Frankie. My hands hurt a bit." This was meant as a small joke, but Frankie immediately began to examine them. We were interrupted by the office door opening. Hamm came out with Mr Moore at his shoulder. Hamm was startled by Roxy and Frankie's presence and didn't know quite what to say. He gave a curt nod to Frankie, clearly displeased, but turned to Roxy and told her to leave.

"It's alright Mr Hamm," said Frankie, "we were seeing if Morrison needed any medical help."

Hamm's eyes came out of their sockets to the point where they dropped out and rolled across the floor. Frankie quickly followed up. "So we'll leave, and I'll take Roxanne back to her class. C'mon Roxy."

Roxy gave my shoulder a rub and left with Frankie, while Hamm ushered me into the office.

It had been a while since I'd been in Mr Moore's office for various trouble I'd found myself in. The last time was when I was organising our interview. Hamm ordered me to stand in front of him and Mr Moore. They both sat at Mr Moore's desk. Hamm looked like he'd been starving but had come across a roast leg of lamb ready for the gorging. Mr Moore appeared smaller than usual, no frown, no smile, not my well learnt neutral face—just one that had come to the end of the road. Hamm assumed the leadership role. "You're lucky you didn't kill the other boy. What did you think you were doing?! We thought of calling the police but decided not to. Of course the boy's parents might think otherwise, but that's up to them. Because of his involvement he's been given a week's 'holiday'." Hamm smirked at his little joke. "But you on the other hand should be expelled."

Up to this point Mr Moore had sat expressionless. I stood there. I had no words, and certainly no explanation—not one I was prepared to share with Hamm at any rate.

Mr Moore finally leant forward and said, "Is there anything that went on, son? Something that could explain what you did?"

Hamm shifted around in his seat, unhappy that the old guy had even suggested that there might be something that would lessen the punishment about to come my way. I said nothing. Not that there wasn't a heap of stuff I could say about my (and others') nemesis. However, even in my furnace of a brain could I say, 'he's a mongrel, been getting in kids' faces for years, making life for people like Petticoat Boy a misery, he deserved everything he got.' Because I could still see some of the distorted images that overpowered me and turned me into a raging bull. Most of which had nothing to do with Chris. Mind you I didn't feel sorry at all for Chris. It was about time somebody belted the crap out of him.

But I could find no reply to Mr Moore. Hamm stood up with a malevolent sneer and said, "Does it have anything to do with him calling you by your real name, *Norman Healey*?!"

Hamm could and should thank his lucky stars that Mr Moore was there as well. Otherwise he might've been sent home to his mum to recover. When Hamm said my 'name' Mr Moore also stood up (I heard his knees crack) and said, "I don't think we need to bring that up, Mr Hamm." Turning to me he asked again if there was any specific reason, apart from Chris tormenting Petticoat, that I could raise.

I shook my head. I wanted the whole pile of crap to be done with. If they were going to shoot me, go ahead. If they wanted to put me on trial, go ahead. If they wanted to expel me for life from the entire education system, go-right-ahead!

Poor old Mr Moore. He had to do what he had to do. He would've liked to tell Hamm to leave us, but he couldn't. He would've liked to have sat me down at the little coffee table and offered me a mint and delve into the why's and wherefores—and you know something? If he had, it might have worked. I might've had the best conversation about my life and my head and my attitude and everything else. Hell, I might've even talked about my mother who apparently lay sick and dying somewhere.

"So *Morrison* (Mr Moore emphasised my name as if rebuking old pig face). This is not what I hoped for but I'm afraid we'll have to suspend you for two weeks. And when you return we'll have to have a talk with your Home Group teacher and your grandmother as well." He turned to Hamm. "Will that be sufficient Mr Hamm?"

Hamm drew in a deep breath. He looked daggers at me as if to say, "Don't we have a dungeon we can put him in?", but he had no more words. Yes I'd copped it, but nothing was going to satisfy him.

Mr Moore looked at me with such sadness, if I was going to cry it would've been then. "Better go and collect your things, son and you can leave the school now. Not a good idea for you to hang around when the rest of the school's going home." Hamm got up and left. Mr Moore allowed himself an exhausted sigh. I got up and went to leave but I stopped at the door and turned to look at my old Principal. "I'm sorry, Mr Moore. I really am. Not for Chris. Not for Mr Hamm. I'm sorry I put you through this. You coulda done without it."

Did he have tears as I left?

Probably.

Did I?

Can't remember. Maybe I did.

CHAPTER ELEVEN

I had been given occasional 'holidays' (hey Hamm, how funny are you?) in the past but it seemed this time I was on the verge of an expulsion. Expulsion was something I didn't want or need. You'd think that I'd be the kind who didn't give a fat rat's if I was thrown out or not but for some reason that wasn't an avenue I wanted to go down. I had begun writing a lot more, some of my efforts had been read by Frankie, mainly because he accepted them as schoolwork assignments, and Roxy, who insisted that I start handing over my writing pieces. By now you'd understand that I wasn't going to refuse her—it would be like commanding a run-away locomotive to stop, simply because you were standing on the tracks. As well, our work in Media had intrigued me and got me thinking but as I got off the bus on that fateful day, my strange friendship with Mr Moore kept running through my head, like a mouse that had escaped its little wheel to find that it was still trapped in a cage. And I think that's the first time I've used the word 'friend' when talking about the old guy.

What makes a friend? When do you know someone is a friend, your friend? Most people don't even think about this question, in fact they wouldn't know that the question exists, much less ask it. Mr Moore had just chucked me out of school, not forever but for a sizeable time, so is that the kind of thing a friend does? My life experience had not provided me with other kids who could naturally become my friend. I mean, I was never in one place long enough for this to happen and I didn't know the way to go about it. In the few kinders I attended the others raced to sandpits and tip trucks and dolls and spades and swings and slides while I stood there wondering how to go about it. But that's not right. I simply stood there without the wherewithal to think about what or how to do it. I stood there amidst all the laughing and giggling and arguing and crying—until a carer would take me by the hand and lead me into some activity. One of the best aspects to these brief experiences was afternoon sleep because when I lay down, the sheets were clean, and the little bed was comfy and cosy.

So if Mr Moore was a friend, how did I know this? I enjoyed seeing him. I liked his chats. I wondered why he'd not painted me into a corner, like you'd expect from a man in his position. He was in a heap of trouble in his own life, but he didn't use that as an excuse to make others miserable. In some ways I suspected it had made him more understanding, more sympathetic. And I didn't share any love of a particular sport with him—I'd been slowly sucked into Grandma's vortex of footy and the Dogs, but Mr Moore could take it or leave it. Although he was passionate about cricket. He'd played cricket and was a fan of Test Cricket which I didn't get at all.

So all I've got with Mr Moore was an old bloke who had simply listened to me, chatted now and then and come to think of it, had saved me from execution, especially from Hamm and the Riverside College Committee of Cruel and Unusual Punishments (Hamm as President, Cottrell as Vice-president and Ms Jacobs, the head librarian as Secretary). Is that enough for someone to be your friend? Probably not. But I did, after all, know a fair bit about him. He was old, gentle, kind of conservative, soon to retire, wife named Jenny who has Alzheimer's, daughter Michelle who lives up north and doesn't seem to visit too often and he loved camping with Jenny. Camping? Now there's something I definitely did not share with him—sleeping on the ground, ants, bugs, beetles, spiders, campfires, freezing your bum off, mud, dirt, crapping in the bush—fair dinkum, no chance of sharing that with anybody, much less Mr Moore.

Thinking about it, Mr Moore had shown a lot of himself, his deep-down-in-the-sea thoughts, his fears, sadness and joy, which had all emerged from those years since Year Eight sitting outside his office, then later shooting the film, and doing the interview. As I walked in my front door, I realised it was those intangibles, those wisps of smoke, those trails of mist that determined who was your friend.

However, my Grandma was not a friend. She was my grandmother, possibly more valuable than a friend. When I told her of my execution, she said, "Oh good Lord, make me a cup of tea and tell me everything." When I finished, her first question was, "You mean you're suspended for two weeks?" Her second question was, "Do I really have to go up to the school with you when you return?" I nodded, "Fraid so Grandma."

"Oh Morrison, you know how those things confuse me. Can't I just ring them and tell them you've promised to be a good boy? That you've done all your homework? That you've painted the house for me? That you've sworn that you'll never hurt another student, even if they're as nasty as the one you nearly put in hospital?"

I grinned. "Don't think that'll work but you could tell them I've been going to church with you—because I obviously need it."

Grandma narrowed her eyes. "Very funny my boy, even if you do need it. I think Walter's starting to like it so there's hope for everybody." I headed off to my room when Grandma said, "That man Kevin rang. Your mother is still in hospital. Doesn't look like she'll get out. Walter says I should go and see her. What do you think?"

I couldn't reply. I didn't have any words. I left Grandma with no answer, entered my room, closed the door and smashed my fist into the bedhead. The bedhead represented no-one. Merely a bedhead that deserved a good beating.

I had never taken Roxy to Buckland's Jetty. I'm a bit warped like that. Don't tell people much. Don't share much. I suppose that makes me secretive, a little paranoid. I mean who would care that Buckland's Jetty means so much to me? Would kids like Chris hate me so much that if they heard about Buckland's they'd blow it up just to annoy me? Highly unlikely. Would others secretly follow me to my special spot? Why would they care? So I know, I suppose that I'm a bit ridiculous about my privacy. Which is why I called Roxy.

"How are you, Morrison? How you going?"

"Great! Excellent! Thought I'd drop around to Chris' place—see how he is."

"For God's sake Morrison. Can you stop being a smartarse for once."

"OK. OK. I'm OK. Kind of... but I was calling to see if you wanted to meet up. Something I want to show you. Can you meet me at the footy oval?"

Silence on the end of the phone. "Roxy? You there?"

"I'm here. Just a bit taken aback—something you want to show me? You mean you're actually going to disclose some part of your life that I know nothing about? This'll be interesting. Sure I'll come. What time?"

"About 10:30. Tonight."

"10:30!! Jees mate. OK. Dunno what I'll say to my parents but OK."

At the appointed time my mate Roxy appeared. It was a coolish night, so we started walking straight away.

"Where are we going, anyway?" she asked.

"I'd rather just show it to you."

"What the hell, Morrison. Out at 10:30. Probably going to freeze our bums off. Almost had an argument with my parents because I had no idea where we were going. Oh yeah, the only way they said yes was if I invited you around for dinner— soon!"

My heart jolted. Meeting the folks! Christ. Me and Roxy were great mates—why couldn't that be enough. It was hard enough for me to find my way in the world without the added bits and pieces of… of… stuff like this. I guessed it would make most people nervous. Like Grandma told me about the first time Grandpa came for a meal to her parents. He was so nervous, he kept burping, trying to answer their questions with mouthfuls of food and to cap it off, sent the peas flying across the table when he was cutting his meat. His final act was telling them he barracked for the Doggies, the very team that had beaten her father's team in the Grand Final that year!

I didn't answer Roxy, just pulled my hood up and kept walking. In half an hour we were at the jetty. Buckland's Jetty. My small space where I came to settle my head and body. In some ways it was like my little chapel. Sometimes I'd sit there for an hour listening to the sea birds and the night birds and the tide gently swishing the sea grass under the jetty, to and fro. If nobody was there, the only exception being my Māori fisherman friend, I'd talk to myself. Don't believe those who say if you talk to yourself it's the first sign of madness. I reckon if you don't talk to yourself you're well on the way to becoming certifiably crazy. And I know Grandma agrees with me considering how many times I've heard her having a chat with herself, and she's one of the sanest people I know.

We walked along the thick, grey boards which thumped and groaned with every step.

"This it?" Roxy asked.

I nodded. "My place, Rox. Can't tell you how often I've come here. Not always if my head's stuffed or if my old mate sadness is hanging around. Sometimes it just gives me some peace when I know it's me and no-one else. Except for an old fishy who comes here, I can imagine being the last person on the planet."

Roxy laughed quietly and turned that smile of hers on me. "Hell Morrison if you're the last person left I'd say the planet's in trouble." She laughed again, pleased with her teasing.

"Roxy, I've told you before, leave the sarcasm to me. It takes years of training."

We reached the end of the jetty, with one lone seagull wheeling in the night sky. Roxy looked around at the sleepy houses behind us and the blue neon and orange lights of the city across the Bay.

"Didn't you write something about this place for English? Early in the year?"

"Yep."

"Thought so but you never showed that one to me." She looked up and put her arm around me. "Thanks Morrison. It's wonderful. It's… got such a stillness to it." She looked across at the city and I had to tell her. Tell her about my fantasy of swimming to the other side of the Bay. Into the dark water, out into the currents, cross the shipping lanes, swimming for my life…

We sat there for some time, no talk, no questions, no answers. Me and Roxy, arms around each other, breathing the salty air. A lone Pacific gull squawked but disturbed nothing.

Roxy looked at me and then out past the yachts, tinnies and dinghies, right across the bay. "Wanna go for a swim?"

"What!?"

"Swim. You know, you get in the water and move your arms like a propeller," she giggled, giving me a push in the chest. "Come on. How many other boys do you reckon I invite swimming?"

I looked at the water. It was like black silk, indistinguishable from the night.

"OK. Bloody cold but."

Roxy was already taking off her jeans and top. I was busy watching her when she said, "Alright, mate. Get your eyes off me and get 'em off". My loud laughter echoed in the streets behind us.

"Shutup, Morrison. You want everybody to join our pool party."

We stood there in our underwear. Roxy had a bright pink bra and green knickers with orange lightning bolts. Even under her clothes she liked to make a statement. "Do we climb down this ladder?" she asked, shivering in the small breeze whispering off the water.

"I'll go first," I said, stepping onto the first iron rung. I had to go first. She was already making me feel like a little wuss.

I slid into water so arctic my balls disappeared, which I hoped and presumed would return later. The iciness was easier to cope with because I could watch Roxy, as she slowly descended the ladder. Before she slipped into the water I noticed a small tatt high up on her thigh. Yeah I know you're thinking about a fish, a mermaid, a dolphin, tinkerbell... but none of that. I could just make out the outline of what looked like a camera.

"So what's the tatt, Rox? Didn't know you did that."

"Don't tell you everything, Morrison. Have to keep a few secrets. From you as well as my parents."

"Is that what I think it is? A camera?"

Roxy swam over to me, spouting water into my face. "Why? Do you reckon I should have a picture of you?! Actually it's a Blackmagic to be precise."

My laughter bounced off the hulls. I had to give it to her. Once she was onto something she was onto it.

"C'mon," she said, striking out towards the outer moored boats. I swam next to her. I enjoyed mixing up my strokes, freestyle, breaststroke, until we reached the last yacht before open water. I rolled over and floated on my back, looking up at the clear night sky, the Southern Cross and its two pointers, and at the other end of the Milky Way, Orion the Hunter. "Float on your back," I said.

But she didn't move, hanging onto ropes dangling from the yacht. "Come on, mate," I urged. I swam over to her and trod water. "What's up?"

Even in the dark she seemed embarrassed. "Look, Morrison, I just don't want to." I reached out and grabbed one of the ropes hanging from the boat.

"I don't know, Morrison. I know I said let's go for a swim but now I'm a bit... scared... you know. Everything's dark. The water. The night. God knows what's below us."

It surprised me a bit. She was always so tough, defiant, devil-may-care. I moved closer to her. I could see her face now, a small smile, water dripping from her hair, beadlets of water on her eyelashes. I pulled her closer to me and kissed that luscious mouth of hers. Lucky for me she didn't push me away, but instead wrapped her free hand round the back of my neck and kissed me, not like the last time for our grand performance at school... maybe a little, but this time I didn't experience a performance, rather a kiss that was full and just for us. A kiss that made me forget to hang onto the rope and sink under the water, abruptly stopping our passion. I spluttered and grabbed the rope again.

"Nothing like ruining our moment. You want to swim back now?" I said.

Roxy's face was so close I could see the green in her eyes. "No, not right now," then she drew me to her so closely there was no water between us. Only her and me. We could've been swept out by the currents. Snatched by giant pelicans. Hunted by sharks. I have no idea how time and space went and who could care. Roxy and I didn't, that's for sure.

Later we walked home along the dark suburban streets of Ballantyne, damp clothes and warm hearts, arms around each other, and for once, we didn't speak a word.

CHAPTER TWELVE

The email concerning my suspension was sent to me and Grandma, outlining my crimes and the duration of my time out. A few teachers sent me work, Jack Kettle, Bernie, Frankie, Izzy—no surprises there. But emails from a young librarian, who informed me of a new book, a new collection of old short stories by John Morrison, had been bought by the school library; and one from Ms Gerrard, my Lit teacher, really surprised me. The Librarian, because she must have done so under the watchful gaze of Commandant Jacobs, and Ms Gerrard who almost certainly had not shared her communication with her secret boyfriend, Hamm. It felt as though there was some forgiveness in the air, something I had not experienced before, which meant I was suspicious. Yeah, OK, my suspiciousness was becoming tiresome, even to me, so I figured I'd do the work they sent me as a gesture to their good intentions.

So much happened in that year, my view of the world was changing. It would have been easy for me to see any kindness as more thinly veiled charity to the 'obviously disturbed Morrison', but I couldn't and didn't. It might have been due to my experiences with Mr Moore; or getting 'shit off my liver' (believe it or not, that's one from Grandma) with writing; or finally belting Chris; or times with my misfit mates, Marcus and Terry; or the movie and the interview; or... moments of passion with Roxy, who was maybe, perhaps, possibly changing from 'a friend with no benefits' to one who I wanted benefits from. Whatever the reason, I thought at that time that there had been enough events and happenings for one year. It was as if I had been on a roller coaster which didn't simply go up and down, eventually coming to a halt back on terra firma. Instead it was a wild ride where there were loops and curves that never went downwards but continued to go up and up to who knows where. I had an inkling more was in store. The year had still more lessons to impart.

I didn't think my having dinner at Roxy's house was a lesson to be learnt; however it was something I didn't relish. She had no brothers or sisters so at least I didn't have to cope with a little brother called, Clarence who insisted on showing me his stamp albums, not to mention his coin collection. All I had were THE PARENTS. I've heard it's hard for most young people to meet 'the folks' but multiply that ten-fold and you'll have an idea of what this walk to Roxy's was like for me. I had experienced anxiety a few times in my life so expected the well-known sweats and short breathing as I trod my way to greetings of 'so this must be Morrison'. I'd already copped some savage teasing from Grandma: 'remember Morrison. No belching, talking with your mouth full and try and not send the peas shooting all over the table'. From Walter I received the suggestion that I could always start off with Alzheimer's jokes. Hilarious!

I rang the bell of an impeccably restored Victorian cottage with a second floor extension at the back. I briefly thought of hiding behind the cars in the street, but I heard running feet in the hallway and then the door was flung open by Roxy, who hugged me before I had a chance to say, 'sorry I've got Dengue fever. Can't make it tonight.' She kept on hugging while her mum and dad came up behind her saying, "Well if you can let go of him for a minute, you could introduce us."

Roxy laughed self-consciously, stopped hugging, but still held my hand and did the introductions.

Her mother said, "Oh you look so hot, Morrison (and she didn't mean 'hot'—she was Roxy's mother, for god's sake). Did you have far to walk? Better come in and get a cool drink."

Her Mum, Debbie was a primary school teacher and her dad, Sam was a builder. They insisted I call them by their 'first' names. Grandma preferred the old term, 'Christian' names but I argued with her, and Walter one night why should we hang onto that when there were many different religions in the country, including Jedi Warriors, not to mention atheists. This was not an argument I had to have with Debbie and Sam. They were, what Grandma would call, 'modern parents'. As far as that night went, it was pretty good. Not too many difficult questions except my suspension, which was raised by Roxy. When I looked at her, she exclaimed, "It's fine. I told them already. Anyway, Dad got expelled from a private school for riding his motorbike on school grounds."

Sam chuckled as much to himself as to us. "Best thing to happen to me. Dad sent me to an old Tech school where I fell in love with carpentry." Carpentry? Mr Moore hovered into view.

The only other touchy subject was: "So Morrison. Roxy tells us that you live with your grandmother. Are your parents still around?" Debbie served more spaghetti onto my plate. Roxy shot a look at her mum. "Hope that's not too personal."

I swallowed and took a drink of mineral water. "No that's OK. One's not around at all and my mother is very sick." My answer so brief, a silence fell over the table, like a dark spectre. I stared at the salad, deep into the bowl, right into the lettuce, tomatoes, celery, cucumbers, onion until they blurred, and my mother appeared, not as in my usual images, but as a patient, dressed in a pink nightie, staring upwards. How long this lasted I have no idea, but I faintly heard Roxy telling them that I liked writing. That I was a good writer. I fished myself out of the salad bowl and grinned like a dying cat.

"Well," said her mother, "we hope you'll let us read some of your work, sometime."

"Took him ages to show me, so good luck with that." Roxy took the salad bowl and put it on the bench in case I tried to dive into it.

Her father saved the moment by asking me what team I barracked for. Thank god. An easy question.

"Oh I go for Doggies. I didn't get to choose. Grandma made it very clear. She might've even thrown me out of the house if I'd gone for any other team."

"Hah! Excellent!" Sam boomed. "Maybe you could come with me and Roxy to a game. Roxy had no choice either." Sam's attitude to me relaxed considerably as he tried to begin a footy conversation with me.

"Oh for heaven's sake, Sam. Let him be." Debbie turned to me. "We agree on many things, Morrison, but even though I love footy I don't let it take over my life. Do I Sam?"

Sam looked sheepish and began clearing the table with Roxy, softly whistling the Doggies' theme song. Well at least I didn't stuff it up like my Grandpa.

"Wanna come watch telly?" Roxy asked. "We can watch it in my room—that way you won't be sucked into a footy chat with Dad." This was one of those situations where my huge lack of experience of other families meant I had no idea whether to say, 'great idea, let's go and make out', or 'thought we could help with the washing up', or simply remain silent. The latter was my choice. Debbie relieved me of my quandary.

"Off you go and I'll bring you in some dessert later."

Of course we didn't go to her room, take off our clothes and jump into bed. Not that we didn't want to. Not even me, in my most I-don't-give-a-stuff mood would have done that. I don't think I would've, at any rate. But walking home that night, I thought about Roxy, Debbie and Sam living happily, going to work, loving their daughter, sleeping in warm bedrooms, knowing each other's strengths and weaknesses... seemed happy enough. All together. Some kind of a family.

I arrived home, the house in darkness. I crept down the hall, past Grandma's bedroom. I stopped and looked in. Grandma snuggled up in her doona, sleeping the sleep of the good and kind-hearted, and I realised that she was my family. OK—we didn't have a husband and wife, siblings crawling over the furniture, the normal family festivities, on and on.

We didn't have the classic Christmas card photo where all is calm, all is bright, but we had such ties of fondness and resilience that I didn't want what Roxy and others had, even though her family was fine. I fell into bed that night, knowing I had something way better than I could've had, something that was like a safety net under a trapeze artist, something that allowed me to swoop and swing and tumble through the air, providing me with a safe landing if I went one somersault too many.

One somersault too many? But what if life does too many? What if you wake in the morning and hear Grandma up too early, dressed up, sitting at the kitchen table, sipping a cup of tea. An absent look in her eye. I gave her my regular good morning hug. "No toast Grandma? Want me to get it?"

She smiled a smile that meant nothing. Or maybe everything.

"Don't think I could keep it down, dear. Even my tea's not hitting the spot." Grandma got up and tipped the dregs down the sink. "Did you have a nice time at Roxanne's?"

I sat down at the table and munched on my toast and peanut butter. "So do I have to ask why you're up and all dressed in your finery?"

She looked out the window, hands on the sink. "I'm going to visit your mother in hospital. Kevin rang me. Apparently she's not improving. They don't expect her to get out of hospital."

That was enough to make me stop eating. Grandma turned and looked at me, a resigned look on her face. "I presume you don't want to come. Walter's coming with me... if that makes a difference."

As I look back on this I see a boy, not a young man, leaving his grandmother's question unanswered. I hear a car's horn outside. Watch Grandma, a squished handkerchief in her hand, gather her bag and walk out, her agonisingly slow footsteps up the hall, the front door closing so softly all you can hear is the click. And then the boy, leaving his toast uneaten, walks to his room, slumps down on a chair in front of his computer, his head drooping onto the keys.

I don't know how long I sat there like that. I literally don't know. A minute. Three hours. As long as I wasn't a part of what was going on at that very moment between my grandmother and her daughter. What brought me back to planet earth was the ding of a text from Roxy, little Terry and Petticoat:

School's not good without you, Morrison.

I think you might be in the minority there, my friends, I texted back. Minority or not, in my eyes they were a formidable group of three who I'd be happy to have next to me if I was ever in a tight spot. The text had woken me from whatever slumber I'd been in and alerted me to a few emails waiting for me. They were all from teachers giving me work. Frankie, what a champion, had invented an assignment he knew I'd like. '*Write whatever's in your head.*' Then he added, *I'm the only one reading it.*

Izzy suggested I might write another synopsis for a movie. While Bernie asked me to write out that whole, 'two plus two stuff' I'd entertained him with. He wanted to send it off to some Maths Teachers Journal—go figure.

Bernie's was easy. I knocked that off in thirty minutes. Then I thought that the tasks of Izzy and Frankie were pretty similar, so I thought I'd kill two birds with one stone. Before I knew it, my head was no longer full of, 'why didn't I go with Grandma, my mother's dying—no matter what she'd done, or, more accurately, what she hadn't done—I should at least see her, look at her, see if she looks how I remember her; why should I see her, just because she's dying, doesn't mend all the damage, if I saw her would I say anything, would I yell at her, could I bear to be near her, stand next to her, hold her hand…'

I'd been saved by schoolwork—yes schoolwork—and so had my bedhead which I had seriously considered beating to a pulp. But there'd been enough bashing and beating and smashing and clobbering and slamming and whacking. I'd seen enough of it and been in the midst of it—and what good had it done me or anybody else? There had been times where it might've done me some good, like looking after myself, but as a rule, it led to an emptiness of heart, of mind, of spirit. So barren nothing grew or swayed, or breathed, smiled or frowned. It was like, one way was life and the other was death.

I sat looking at my cursor. Blink. Blink. Blink. Then, slowly, the words spoke to me and began to spill onto the page with the imaginative title of:

Life and Death

We live, we die. That's the deal. It's the deal for us as well as blades of grass, elephants, friends and enemies alike. It's the deal made before we yawn, stretch and slide out of our mothers' wombs. Who makes this deal I have no idea, but it probably goes like this:

Next!

So you want to be born?

OK that's fine. There's a few thousand wanting the same thing today. Don't know whether they'll get what they want but we'll do our best. Let's deal with the humans first. The blades of grass and elephants will have to wait.

Now the one thing you'll have to think about before you leap into the void is that Life is not a bunch of roses. It can be but it often isn't. But that's not the real rub of the whole shebang. The question you have to think about, and answer is, if you live, do you realise and accept that the other part of this deal, a dualism if you will, that you will die? Dead! Deady Bones! Gone! Passed on! Passed Away. Passed.

Of course you accept that. I mean, it's so far away, that death-part of the deal. When you start asking the unanswerable, maybe when you're four or five, you don't get any satisfaction at all. You get answers like, 'oh don't worry, by the time you get old they'll have all kinds of things that will make you live forever'. What the adult doesn't realise is that you're not asking about living forever, you're asking the fundamental question: how come we have to die and what happens after? Any parent, grandparent, old uncle can only give the answers they've got, which is bugger all. It's not their fault, they've had to deal with it whatever way they can. Death is a burden, mainly because as far as we know, we humans are the only sentient beings on the planet that know from the outset that we're going to die.

Which brings me to religion, the mainstay of those trying to answer what happens later. Every single religion, the main ones, plus their offshoots, plus the wackos all have an answer. All of them work on the principle of an afterlife, a spirit, a prophet, a god, or a God that is responsible for Life and Death. I once heard a bloke on the telly say that the only two reasons for religion was one, to control our sexual urges and two, help us deal with death. Mmmm. From what I can see, the first one hasn't worked and the second only works if you're a true believer, like my Grandma.

I wonder how the great Superior in the Sky would have reacted when he or she first heard that their job was to help humans deal with Life and then, Death.

'Whaaaat?! So the job entails providing answers about life and death. I don't know whether I have the knowledge or experience to do that. I mean, I know I'm 'The Almighty' but that's pushing the job description a bit far. Ask me about weather, famine, floods, pestilence—now I've got a handle on those—but the Big Question? Can't somebody else do that? Isn't there anybody higher than me who could and should be the answer to all that. Honestly, you guys take the cake. You told me it was a straightforward job and that I was the ONLY one who could fill it.'

Would you take on that job? I know I wouldn't. Although I would have liked to ask the big questions myself, when I was a *little tacker living somewhere, in some house, in some place. It would've been nice to ask my mother, or even one of her special friends, those simple little questions that roam through little kids' minds, often as they lie in bed or when confronted by the death of someone in their life. I can only presume there must've been deaths in my mother's life, but nothing comes to mind.*

But my mother's death now comes to my mind. Did she ever have the chance, even the joy of asking those questions to Grandma and Grandpa, lying in bed, wondering about Life and what lay in store? If she did, I doubt that she would've thought she would end up in hospital, dying almost alone, too young to die, a nasty death as her organs begin to throw in the towel. I doubt she would have dreamt of having her own little boy who would ask those questions of her. I doubt that little boy would enter her thoughts. As I write this I doubt it, but I also find myself wondering if she would think of me. I find myself hoping that she would think of me.

I find myself taken by surprise that I can think softly about my mother. Probably too late to visit. Too late to ask her about Life and what happens when we die.

Morrison.
11B.

Looking back, I remembered two things two teachers told me. Jack Kettle once said that writing was an act of discovery. You start out writing and you think you know what you want to say but as you write you discover other truths that float to the surface. Stan of 'Stan and Izzy' fame said to me and Roxy that all creativity looks at the questions of life and death. It's not forced, he added, it's just there, whether you know it or not.

I'll have to think further about what Stan said, but Jack Kettle was on the money. If you don't believe me, just read my piece on 'Life and Death'. And look where I ended up.

I read it through and before I came up with all the excuses, I sent it off to Frankie, with the reminder that it was for his eyes only. Then I sent it to Roxy with the same warning. I got up from my desk, feeling jittery and strangely light as well. I went outside to check if Grandma and Walter had returned. I went back in and got a drink from the fridge. Then I returned to my desk and sent it to Izzy, explaining that I wasn't sure if this was suitable for a movie but maybe Roxy could see something I couldn't.

Without warning, my fingers working without me, I sent my writing to Mr Moore. I didn't tell him to keep it to himself. I knew he would. Except I added a note: *Dear Mr Moore. Letting you know that I'm gainfully occupied. Morrison.*

I owed him that much.

CHAPTER THIRTEEN

Yes I did owe Mr Moore heaps. School would not have held me if it hadn't been for him. I've tried to put a finger on it, to define what it was about him that I saw, felt and responded to. It's like those words I've put down about what makes a friend. It seems the more words you put on it, the more distant you get from the answer. It's like shooting the ducks at the sideshows. Seems easy until you line them up, miss the lot and of course miss out on the big brown teddy bear. So when I think of Mr Moore, I fall back on generalities—kindness, understood me, clearly saw my defences, loving to his wife—so on and so on. None of that captures what he was like and how I felt. Reading through what I've put down so far, I see it's the whole story, what he did and said, what I did and what I said, that is the only way to go close to my time with Mr Moore. Perhaps it was his sense of forgiveness that turned a light on in my brain. The light which began as a tiny blipping glow, quickly became a row of incandescent lights, then changed to thousands of Catherine wheels fizzing and sparking on the Sydney Harbour Bridge.

Grandma had not said much since her hospital visit. (See—that's what I'm like. Can't even say straight out, 'since seeing *my mother* in hospital'.) I'd been around to see Roxy—always a good experience but also to make sure there were no other guys sniffing around. You gotta watch other guys. They'll move in on you faster than you can say, 'you're dumped!'—friends included, although my main friends were little Terry and Petticoat and no matter how feverish my imagination can get, neither one of them was about to jump on Roxy.

A day after Grandma had done her visit TO MY MOTHER (that felt good) I sat with her in the early evening as she watched her diet of quiz shows and then her battery of news and news magazine programs. Einstein sat at her feet, looking after her and probably answering the quiz questions as well. "You should watch more news Morrison. Good idea to know what's happening in the world. Truth as well as lies." I smiled at her, then, with some effort, I asked the question stuck in my belly.

"Grannie. How was it the other day?"

It was all I could manage.

Grandma cast a quick look at me and went back to the TV. She said nothing for some minutes. It seemed like I wasn't the only one who had problems with speaking the unspeakable. She kept her eye on dreadful attacks in some Middle Eastern country, took a sip of her sherry, and still without looking at me, said, "Hardest thing I've done in my life, love. I didn't recognise her. She probably couldn't recognise herself either. She was paler than pale and wasn't really on the ball at all. I said hello and there was a second where I think she recognised me. Walter told me he saw her smile but that's just Walter, forever the optimist. Maybe she did… I'd like to think she did." Grandma took another sip and sighed, a sigh from yawning depths, from places I recognised. She continued staring at the screen without seeing. "I'm glad I went though. Poor girl. Poor Cheryl… my poor daughter." Hearing my mother's name jolted me. Grandma twisted the rings around on her fingers and finally looked at me. "Morrison, there are some things in life where even if you went back in time you couldn't make a difference. I've berated myself for years about what went wrong, how did it happen, how did things get out of hand so quickly?" She reached for the tissues next to her. "I know you think your Grandma's got life sorted but there are things that will never be sorted." She went back to the news. "I'm sad. I feel terrible. I thought one day I might have my darling grandson having Sunday roasts with his mother at my home… but not to be… At least we're not as badly off like those poor buggers." She pointed at the telly. "We don't have chemicals and bombs raining down on us, day in and day out."

I saw that her glass was empty. "How about I get you another one, Grandma. I don't think it'll hurt your diabetes." She smiled. When I returned I sat down again, took her hand and asked one of the hardest questions of my life. "Is it too late to see her... I mean... should I... you know, go into the hospital?"

"To tell the truth, I don't know. She looks terrible and they say she could die any day now. I don't think I can do it again. I'm sorry my darling boy. Perhaps Walter?"

I had nothing against Walter. He'd brought some sunshine into Grandma's life. And what's more, never pretended to be my grandfather nor give me sage advice simply because he was old. But the hospital thing? That was mine and mine alone to do. If I wanted to.

I returned to my room. I didn't text, email, chat, phone, write—nothing. I lay on my bed and stared at the ceiling, just the way my mother was doing at that very minute. I thought of people like Grandma in my life. Frankie. Roxy. Terry and Marcus. Stan. Izzy. And of course, Mr Moore. None of them rejected me because of the stories they'd heard, nor what I'd done, nor my reputation that had gone before me. They could have easily done so but they didn't. They offered... something... kindness? Interest? Succour? When I thought of them they all faded and moved out of the way as the spectre of Mr Moore floated into view. He knew I could be a little arsehole. He knows that. He knew that. And yet...

I got up from my bed, gave the bedhead a dark look, went into the lounge room, kissed Grandma and walked out of the house, caught a bus to the Western General Hospital, got off and stood on the opposite side of the road in the shadows, looking up at a five storey cream brick building that was at present, home to my mother. The night was cold and the trams screeching and cars beetling along made it feel colder, and the hospital more forbidding. I pulled up my hoodie and slouched against a street pole. I looked up and counted the floors—1, 2, 3, 4, 5—I knew she was on the fifth. Grandma said she was in Ward 5D, but I couldn't figure which room it might've been from the lights shining from the row of windows. The Emergency sign stood out against the traffic lights, shops and car lights. I figured that's where she must have been taken some days ago, probably by Kevin. I wondered why Kevin had stuck by her. I wondered why he'd taken it upon himself to take me to Grandma's all those years ago. My memories indicated that my mother had never done anything kind and nice nor been a wonderful friend to her changing band of no-hopers. So how come she'd even made it to the hospital? I don't think I would've done it. How come a bloke like Kevin?

Then I saw the very same man emerge from the doors of the Emergency. He wore a big, padded jacket which he zipped up against the cold, searched his pockets, found a cigarette, lit up and drew on it like it was his last. He peered into the night making me shrink back behind the pole. I might've had all those questions, but I had no desire to saunter over the road and say, "Hi Kev. Glad to see you. And tell me, mate, how come you care so much for my mother when she was such a dog?" Not only did I not want to ask the question, I didn't want to hear the answers. Why? Well… to be as honest as I can be in this story, they might've told me some things about her that might have softened my attitude about her, and I wasn't prepared to allow that to happen. Not yet at any rate.

Kevin finished his ciggie, took a look into the shadows where I hid, and walked off. It was quite late, too late for a visit, I told myself. Don't know how long I stood there but something dragged me across the road, right up to the doors of Emergency. Before I knew it, I was inside. Visiting hours were well past and there was me, a nurse, and a cleaner guiding his machine across the polished lino. A big Pacific Islander security guard stood as a sentinel at the lifts, checking his phone. I walked over to the ATM as though I knew what I was doing in there. I fiddled with the buttons:

Require a receipt?

Nah.

Want this as your normal withdrawal amount?

Nup.

Transaction fee of $2.00. Accept?

Do I have a choice?

Why are you here?

What?!?

Are you going up to the fifth floor to see your mother?

The screen fired one message after another.

Don't have all day. Do you want a receipt for your visit?

I felt my blood move from simmer to red crayfish boiling. I looked at the ATM with the same glare I gave my bedhead. The guard was now closely checking me out. Not moving but his eyes bored into me. If I wasn't careful the good ol' Morrison might erupt and smash the screen on the ATM. I pretended to take my money and fiddled with my wallet. I smiled at the guard and walked over.

"Visiting hours are over, son. Only close family and if patients are... are... in a bad way..."

He waited, expecting an answer. I stared at the shiny lift doors. A reflection of the guard's colossal back and a young guy who looked smaller than he was.

"Who did you want to visit, son?"

"My mother. She's in 5D. Dying... she's dying." It was out of my mouth before I could bottle it up. "I work at a Supermarket. Just got off work." My reliable pack of lies spilled forth.

The guard put his huge mitt on my shoulder. "OK kid. Better get up there. Make it quick though."

He pushed the button, the door opened and as I walked in he said, "Sorry about your Mum. I lost mine when I was a young man. Look after yourself."

As the lift rose to where I didn't want to go I thought about the guard saying he'd lost his mum. All the different words for death: dead, snuffed it, kicked the bucket, passed, passed away, killed, gone to heaven, and lost—lost? But they're not lost, their loved ones know exactly where they are.

Ding! The doors slid open, and I stepped out into a very quiet ward. Eerily silent, except for the hum and beeping of machines and the two nurses at the desk. I walked over and tried my Morrison charm, what was left of it. They were both young and seemed happy to see another young one. One of them smiled at me, enquiringly. "Ah, sorry for coming at this hour. Had to work. Come to see the patient in 5D." The patient?! Christ I'm stupid sometimes, well a lot of times, but now they had to ask the question: 'Are you a relation?"

I tried to answer straight away, but nothing came out. The nurses looked at me and stopped what they were doing. I pretended to have a coughing fit while I formed the right words in my head. Prickly beads of sweat all over me. "Is she you mother?" one of them asked, her brow furrowing.

I nodded my head a number of times so vigorously I felt and looked like one of those figures on a spring you stick on your dashboard.

"I'll show you where she is. But I'm afraid you'll have to make it short. Sorry."

I smiled weakly and followed with my feet full of lead weights. The nurse stopped at an open door and gestured for me to enter. Again I smiled weakly, and stood at the door looking in.

"You can go in."

I took a quick look inside the room. "Yeah, OK. I will in a minute."

The nurse placed her hand softly on my arm and left. Strange how these strangers felt for me. A guard. A nurse. Couldn't help comparing it to my mother who I couldn't remember showing me such tenderness. I suppose she did, but nothing came to mind.

I finally looked at the unlookable. Three machines, lights on, blues, oranges, blinking. Screens with lines worming their way across the glass. IV tubes, oxygen masks and tanks. All for one human being. All contributing to the life of someone on the bed. I remained at the door and forced myself to look. A woman, surprisingly young looking but the ravages of time, drugs, booze, make-believe happiness, a sadness you couldn't plumb. All there on display, the woman who bore me, no open eyes, the slightest of breath, the palest of skin so ashen and wretched you wondered why she wasn't already dead. My mother. My Mum. For a moment sweats and dizziness returned. I forced another look, took a breath from the depths of the oceans, from the bowels of the earth, all the way in, all the way down, until my whole being was full of what I could see, hear, smell... and remember. I remained at the door, looking away. Why didn't I go in and touch her? Why not say hello to a woman who couldn't hear you and couldn't respond if she did? The only reply was to feel tears free-falling down my face, seeping from my heart, over my body, trickling through time, washing through my life.

I managed to get myself together, on the surface at any rate, and stumbled away from 5D, past the nurses' desk, into the lift, past the guard who I gave a wave to and out into the dark of night. There were plenty of buses, but I only wanted to walk. Which is what I did. All the way home.

How long did it take?

I have no idea.

And guess what?

It rained all the way home.

Perfect.

Chapter Fourteen

Nearly at the end of my suspension, with two days to go, my mother died.

I was in my room, listening to a song from *Dirtbag*, 'Down but not Done', which kept telling us to stop sooking and keep going. Strange how the universe sends us messages, eh? Grandma took the call. I heard a thump and raced into her room to find her collapsed on the floor. I knelt down beside her and cradled her in my arms while she silently sobbed. As she wept, a small moan came from deep within her, or from somewhere else, from some place where humans sometimes go when all is sad and lost and buried, when there are no answers to our predicament, to our deep abiding pain, that goes to the beginning of all things.

I buried my head in her shoulder and cried like a baby with no mother. The tears which refused to fall for so many years, unplugged and never ending. Me and my Grandma in a hopeless bundle on the floor. And then I heard softly spoken words from Grandma which formed into small prayers, unlike those you hear from pulpits but prayers, nonetheless. On the surface, only bits and pieces made sense, but then they all made sense to me. Grandma may have been withering in her talk about her daughter, but she bore her, watched over her, loved her, raised her, saw her leave after Grandpa's death, hoped, wished, and prayed for a different outcome—and bore the pain once again. I didn't begrudge her faith. Whatever gets you through the night.

Walter arrived before I could say, 'mother'. What a good man he was and is. Gentle, caring with one person in mind. He went about looking after her, tending to her needs while I poured her a generous glass of sherry. He sat next to her on the bed while she continued to weep, holding her old brown freckled hand, never once asking her to stop crying. He knew she had a few reservoirs of tears in there. She was in good hands, so I went to my room and lay down but this time no crying, no tears. Not because I felt nothing. In fact I had so many feelings of so many types, genres, forms that I didn't know what to do with them. I was scared of letting them drip out—the droplets would have so quickly become a tsunami that would've washed me away to unknown destinations. Which shows that at least I now knew the tears were there, no matter for how many years I denied their existence.

I called Roxy. I went over to her place after school. We walked to the jetty. She held my hand the whole time, the whole way. I said not one word. She asked not one question. The sea breeze stroked my face, the wind blew the cobwebs from my brain. I was allowed to stay overnight at her place. Walter stayed with Grandma. I guess Kevin sat with my mother until they took her away.

The funeral was at some little known funeral parlour, Partelli and Sons, in the smallest room they had. Kevin, to his credit organised it all and kept Grandma informed. He asked if there was anything she'd like to happen? Anything she'd like to do? Flowers, she wanted to buy lots of flowers, she said. After she hung up she rang back almost immediately and said she'd like to say a prayer. Roxy asked if she could call Petticoat and little Terry. I said no, so quickly and loudly it startled her. She just looked at me. Her looks were her best communication. I knew them. Understood them. So I relented and said OK.

The next two days were a blur. I have no idea what I did, who I saw, who I hid from, what I thought about. This is not the easy avoidance it sounds like. I literally can't remember a thing about the days leading up to the funeral. I wish I could because somewhere in that time I sank to the depths of the ocean, not in despair, not to the land of the black dog—more where I holed up, hunkered down, allowed whatever it was that I was feeling to wash over me, enter me, hold me. I think it was some days of slow but imperceptible calmness, like a raging storm had become a smooth rolling ocean, a wild beast had soothed itself. When I emerged from this chrysalis I had not turned into a butterfly nor a born-again human being, but something had been tweaked, sandpapered, restored. I was a little blue and white launch, gently rocking in the harbour, becalmed and safe.

We all went together. Grandma, Walter, me and Roxy in Walter's car. Einstein came along for the ride, happy to be included. Pantelli and Sons was not too far from Buckland's Jetty, which I saw as a good omen. We parked in the funeral parlour carpark, close to the main highway leading to Geelong. The drum of the cars and trucks could be heard as we made our way into the chapel. There were a few others, some surprisingly well-dressed and not looking like the flotsam and jetsam I thought would be there. Of course, there were some like that, but they had at least made an attempt to tidy up. Strange to hear me say that—normally I couldn't give a stuff about clothes and appearances. A couple stayed outside having their last ciggies. Roxy probably needed one but didn't.

Inside, the assigned chapel was small. "Not big enough to swing a cat in," whispered Grandma as we entered. There were four pews, enough room for twenty people but only a dozen turned up. A couple of Grandma's friends from her church were there. Kevin was already there and went straight to Grandma and gave her a kiss on the cheek. She introduced the rest of us. Kevin shook my hand a bit too vigorously, saying, "I know who this fella is. Good to see you, Norman."

Yes, that rankled but I managed a smile and nodded. I felt Roxy hold her breath and then exhale when she realised I wasn't going to blow up. We sat down in the front pew, the casket only two meters away. It was a cheap pine box but nicely polished. I've heard that people can get buried in cardboard boxes and cloth sacks where they lower you in feet first. That is, of course, if you're not getting cremated. I think that's the way I'll go—the idea of being declared dead and then somehow coming back to life, only to discover you're in a sealed coffin, six feet under. Knock knock. Hello. Hello. Anyone there?

Grandma had gone mad with the flowers. They lay all over the coffin and spilled onto the floor. She'd chosen and ordered a wonderful variety—irises, roses, bottlebrush, lilies, and little sprigs of creamy white gardenias, Grandma's favourite, here and there, their tropical perfume wafting over the mourners.

Others began to troop in. None of them I recognised, and none seemed to know who the hell I was, much less the old lady and gentleman sitting next to me. Taped music of a hymn played. Grandma leant over to me and told me what it was— *The Lord's my shepherd*—not exactly Hip Hop but it sounded pretty good and anyway, my world could do with a few more shepherds. I was surprisingly together, and Grandma only dabbed at her eyes with a handkerchief—her special church hanky with embroidered bunches of primroses in the corners. I sat there not wanting to check out the remnants of my mother's friends. Roxy hooked her arm into mine and leant towards me. The minister walked in and as he did I heard movement behind me. I looked around and there was Marcus and little Terry. They smiled and Marcus patted me on the shoulder. Strange. These two and Roxy knew nothing about my mother except they'd picked up that I hated her. So I guess they were there for me—and Grandma.

The minister cleared his throat and asked us to stand, explaining what we were all there for. A bit unnecessary, I thought. He then gave an account of my mother, obviously based on information supplied by Kevin. The minister didn't know her from a bar of soap, but at least he sounded as though he did. Sitting there I gazed at the box that housed what was left of her, while the minister droned on. One of the congregation began to sniffle, then cry, then wail until she was helped out of the chapel. I wondered if I was supposed to feel like that, except my tears weren't there. That's not to say I wasn't overcome. I was. But it was an 'overcome' like I'd been punched senseless and all I could do was 'be'.

The minister asked us to stand again, nodding to Grandma, who, with Walter supporting her, stood out front and reading from a printed sheet, she delivered her prayer:

"We thank you that Cheryl has outsoared the shadow of our night, with its cruelty pain and violence, when the trouble was near, we could not understand, how you seemed to remain far away..."

I'm not sure what tipped me into wonderland. Perhaps it was Grandma praying the words, *'you seemed to remain far away'*, or more likely, the whole damn event but whatever it was, triggered something inside me. I lost my sense of nothingness and stared at the casket. At first it was what it was—a very ordinary pine coffin. But then it became less solid and then, less opaque... the wood panels and lid shimmered, swirled and finally I could see my mother all laid out inside. If she had stayed like that I could've coped. But no. She *had* to open her eyes, stretch and sit up, didn't she? As if she hadn't given me enough grief in my life. They'd dressed her (who were 'they'?) in a light blue top and jeans which must have been bought for the occasion. I seemed to remember her in those clothes. While I glared, not wondering for a second if others could see what I saw, my mother turned to me, and hoisting herself up a few more inches, looked at me. At me?! And gave a pale, winsome little smile: "Hello Norman. OK if I call you that? Heard you changed your name. Not sure if the others here can see what you can but that's alright. You're the one I want to talk to".

I swallowed hard. "You want to talk to *me*?"

"I know. Bit hard to believe isn't it, me wanting to chat right here and now." She moved around in the box, trying to get comfortable, searching for something in her jeans. "Damn," she said, "You'd think they'd put a packet of ciggies in with me. Might be a long trip."

She looked at me again. "Listen Norman. I might not have very long so I'll say what I've got to say and then get out of your life—well, I've already got out of your life once, but I think this time it might be more permanent."

I didn't like her light and breezy attitude. "Actually, you didn't get out of my life," I said. "The way I remember it, you tossed me out of your life."

My mother looked at her nails and then placed a hand on the sides of the coffin. With a crooked smile she whispered, almost to herself, "I deserved that. Yes I did that. And I probably don't deserve one bit of sympathy. Sorry..."

Somehow the apology meant nothing . I felt the molten lava that sat in small reservoirs stir deep inside me. "All these years and now..."

She began to cry, quietly. "I used to get news about you sometimes. A friend had a nephew who went to your school. He said he'd heard you were a bit of a writer. That pleased me. It was about the only thing I liked at school. Wrote some poetry... pretty bad though."

Of course I wanted to tear apart all the words that dribbled from her mouth, to say what you'd expect me to say. To have a go at her about all the obvious stuff I could've spewed up. But what to say to a dead mother who was a terrible mother and now lounged in her own coffin?

"One thing before I go. I always kept a photo of you. Here, it's in my pocket". She fossicked around and pulled out a creased photo of me as a little boy. Yes, again the replies I could've made. But didn't.

"I think your Grandma's finishing up her prayer now, so I better get back in here. I'm sorry, Norman. Would've been a nicer life if you'd been in it. And that's my fault."

She slipped back inside and closed the lid.

I faintly heard the last words of Grandma's prayer, '... *if life is soured by bitterness, an unforgiving spirit brings no peace...*', as my body sagged, drained, emptied, and somebody's hands grabbed hold of me to stop me from collapsing and toppling off the pew. I felt as sick as a dog. Palms so sweaty they were greasy. Head so hot I wondered if it was on fire. Body so putrid I stank.

It was Marcus who'd grabbed me from behind and Roxy who held onto my arm with a vice-like grip and stopped me from shattering into shards of glass memories. I think they were the only ones who saw, not what I had seen, but the effects of my bizarre encounter.

Grandma finished the prayer, and leaning towards Walter, she clutched his arm and said, "I am Cheryl's mother. Except for Kevin, nobody knows that I was and am her mum. Some will know that Cheryl and I hadn't seen each other for many years, which affected me deeply. I can only hope she felt the same way... but possibly she didn't. Whatever the case, no matter how much trouble between us there was, I loved her." Grandma stopped, while the door of the chapel opened for a latecomer. She took a deep breath and staggered a little, "... and who could not love their own child. When I think of her I think of happier times, when her father was alive... but if I have anything to thank her for it was the day Kevin brought her son to me. Morrison has been the light of my life. That was something Cheryl did that made the world a better place. I thank you all for coming."

The minister announced there'd be tea and coffee served. I sat down and exhaled, like I'd been storing it up. Grandma and Walter sidled out of the pew. I turned to thank Marcus and Terry and as I did I saw a man standing at the back of the room. I blinked. Looked again. Shook my head. Wondering if this was another strange apparition. It was Mr Moore—who gave me a smile and walked towards me, stopping to say hello to Grandma and Walter.

"My apologies for being late, Morrison. School. I am very sorry, Morrison." He looked at Roxy, Marcus and Terry, who began to hurriedly explain that he had a note from his mum to attend the funeral. We all laughed at the little hero who was babbling until Mr Moore patted him on the head and assured him he wasn't in trouble. He shook my hand, then the others'. "Your Grandma rang me and told me the sad news. Hope you don't mind. Seemed silly for me not to come." He looked at the four of us and said, "I can still remember the day my Mum died. Tore me and my brother to shreds. I think she was always the anchor of my family... not unlike your grandmother, Morrison." He looked down at the floor. Then, "Well I better get back to school. The whole place might blow up if I'm not there." He laughed at his own little joke. "I'll say goodbye to your folks and leave you to it."

Leave us to it?! The service was strange enough but now I had to go out there and have a drink and see all these people who I may or may not have known. Roxy guided me to the coffee, tea and cakes out in the vestibule. Some were talking to Grandma, as though they knew her. Kevin made a bee line for me and so I had to do the introductions but what I really wanted to say out loud was, "Hey! You guys! My mother just sat up and talked to me. Are you sure she's dead?! I mean, have you checked lately? Anybody heard any knocking?" It occurred to me that some of my mother's friends were so out of it they may have looked at her, said that she looked like she was dead and bought a cheap box and popped her in. Then went back to whatever they were doing.

Kevin prattled on with my friends while I got a cup of coffee. Little Terry eyed the sponge with jam and cream until he couldn't bear it any longer and grabbed a gargantuan slice. I stirred my coffee, the way I normally did. One sugar, bit of milk, stir one way and then the other. Pick it up with my left hand. A man at the end of the room stood with a couple of women. He wore a mauve suit, almost shiny, been ironed one too many times. He chatted but I noticed he never took his eyes off me. He pretended not to but to a trained observer like myself, it was as obvious as the cream all over Terry's face. So I pretended not to notice. I took in everything—as well as the way he was holding his cup of coffee. Yep. Left hand.

I'd had enough for one day. And that's the understatement of the year. Grandma looked as though she wanted to get out of there, so with one last look at the coffin still sitting there all alone, I left with Grandma and friends. I know the question you're most likely screaming from the grandstands, but I don't have much of an answer. Except to say, it was probably him. He didn't take a step in my direction, which I thought he owed me, but I was glad he didn't. And anyway, I'd just had a little chat with my dead mother. Enough's enough.

Chapter Fifteen

Here I was back at school. At the coal face. The place of learning. Education whether you took to it or not. Grandma had been excused from attending my first meeting after a special dispensation from Mr Moore. The meeting, with Frankie, Mr Moore and good ol' Hamm was to ensure I was now a new boy, one who knew better, who promised to turn over a new leaf, who guaranteed that he would never ever smash the life out of any other kid whether they deserved it or not. Frankie of course was the one who came up with the idea that if I ever felt like blowing like a volcano it might be a good idea if I had someone I could say, "Hey, my reservoirs of lava are leaking like a sieve." Frankie offered to be that person. Fair dinkum, Frankie was one of those teachers who I'll probably remember for the rest of my life.

Life went on and a week later Riverside College put on their annual student film festival at the Ballantyne Cinema. Our little movie had been titled, *I know Where I Come From*, although I'd pushed for *The Old Man and the Sea*—Petticoat pissed himself laughing, while Roxy said, "Very funny, but I think it's been used before." Little Terry was non-plussed.

Ballantyne Cinema had been brought back from an early grave and it now had become a landmark of good movies. It was a quaint, art deco building with the word, *Ballantyne Cinema* sitting atop, surrounded by a jagged neon sign resembling a star. You could invite friends and family for the annual awarding of *The Greenbergs*, named after some Screenwriter who worked on Australian movies and TV shows for kids. Apparently, according to Roxy, he was like a god to the film industry. Whatever, all I knew was that Roxy was caught-up in her lust for a prize. I told her that she already had me as her prize but copped a look that kept my laughter to myself.

It was, as they say, the night of nights. Everybody dressed up in their finery, or what they thought of as finery. Teachers who never wore suits, turned up in them. Women who never wore dresses or skirts, turned up in dazzling costumes that turned heads (including me). Students from the film camp outdid themselves, especially the try-hards who wore sunglasses, with the boys in tuxes (for Christ's sake). The stoners turned up straight, mainly due to the presence of their parents. Our little entourage worked hard at being different to the run of the mill—Roxy with a stunning short orange skirt over purple tights that seemed to run all the way up to her armpits (give me a break, she was astonishing); little Terry in a dark suit with a ruffled white shirt (paid for by his single mum who seemed too old to have a kid Terry's age); me with dyed electric blue hair, glasses I didn't need, black jeans, black T-shirt, purple Doc Martins (OK a bit over the top but I didn't want to let the side down); and now the one you've been waiting for, Marcus, Petticoat Boy. At first he looked like the most mundane of us, until you noticed the black eyeliner, the extra piercings on his nose, tongue, bottom lip and around his ears. Where's the petticoat you ask? Had Marcus finally succumbed to society's demands? Of course not. Possibly as a sweetener to his Greek parents, he wasn't actually wearing one but had a bright red petticoat tucked into the belt of his pants which fell to his side like a matador's scarf, making even more of a statement, if that was possible for Petticoat Boy.

It was quite a spectacle. Walter and Grandma in their going-out clothes. Roxy's parents, who looked very cool, who made such a fuss of us when they arrived we wished we weren't there. Then to make it that bit more embarrassing, they insisted on being introduced to Grandma, which I did quickly and immediately entered the cinema before anything else weird happened.

We had to sit with our film crew. That was fine. I looked around at the bulging theatre. So many people. Stan and Izzy running around making sure things were organised. Stan was the master of ceremonies. Most of the teachers sat up the back (force of habit, I reckon. Gotta watch those kids!). I noticed Mr Hamm and Ms Gerrard sat on opposite sides of the cinema. Was that just for appearances or had the bushfires of passion been quelled or had Ms Gerrard finally come to her senses? Lights started to go down but a moment before complete darkness, a figure appeared at the end of our row and asked us to move up. Mr Moore. "Well," he whispered, "they asked us to sit with our film crew." I was beginning to love this old bloke. I'd heard his wife had deteriorated quite quickly and yet here he was. "And anyway," he whispered directly to me, "I might get a prize." Now do you see why, over all these years, that he was the one person, besides Grandma, who knew what made me tick. And probably tock as well!

I won't bore you with the entire proceedings, but there are three short episodes. After the screenings came the awards. We did not get 'best film'. The stoners had managed to dream up a great little movie called, *'Things We Don't See'*, where they filmed ants tunnelling in sand, beetles under leaves, flies in spider webs, spiders being eaten by their lovers, flies feasting on scraps, blowflies on meat complete with maggots, and bees searching for pollen. I felt Roxy's body go rigid with tension, expectation and disappointment. But we did get second and Robbie Greenberg, the judge, and after whom the awards were named, said it was a difficult decision (don't they always say that to who comes second) and then immediately went into our movie declaring that the Director had such a talent for 'seeing' each scene and promptly gave her 'Best Director'. Up Rox went on stage, crowd gone mad and with her father, Sam leading the ovation and whistling like he was at the footy. Roxy didn't seem to mind, she even performed a curtsy and then returned to her seat, clutching her trophy, which was a plastic copy of the Blackmagic. She sat there, smiled at her crew who beamed back but from that time onwards she gripped her prize like it might never leave her side. Fleetingly I thought she might have a new boyfriend and that it would get into her bed before me!

And then up came 'Best Actor'. I looked over at the 'oh dahhhhling' film buffs who could hardly contain their expectations. The girl from the camp who wore flowing velvet dresses and flowing golden locks and flowing narcissism sat on the aisle, with her mates patting her on the knee and telling her to get ready to accept. Greenberg looked at the card given to him by Izzie and smiled. He knew dramatic effect, how long to pause, when to look at the audience. "... the clear winner, for an amazing performance and from a person with no dramatic background, the winner of the 'best actor' goes to, for his performance in, '*I Know Where I Come From*'... Mr Bill Moore!"

Every award before then had met with immediate applause. After this announcement, there were inward sucks of air, silence that was deafening, some wondering who the hell Mr Bill Moore was. Then I stood up and punched the air, whooping and yelling, Petticoat and Terry and Roxy joined me and then the whole bloody place erupted. Students, parents, teachers, general public—all of them, every single person on their feet, lifting the roof off the old cinema. And the funny thing was that there would've been quite a few who would hardly have known who he was and that he was the Principal of Riverside College. Mr Moore hesitated before rising on his creaky knees and almost shuffled up the stairs to the stage. He had to wait for some time before the adulation abated. His speech was very short and very sweet. He thanked 'the crew' (actually used that term with a wink) and for the director for having faith in him (flashbacks of Roxy standing in waist deep water and a hypothermic actor). He began to leave the stage, stopped and nodding at Robbie Greenberg, he returned to the mic. "Sorry. Forgot one thing. Every good film needs a good story. That story was provided by one of our crew, and that person was Morrison. Thank you Morrison, a better story than you will ever know."

Yeah OK. Got some good clapping. I snuck a look back at the audience. Grandma and Walter on their feet. Beaming. Roxy's modern parents. Whistling. Frankie and Jack Kettle. Did I see Hamm on his feet? Nah, let's be serious.

Roxy leaned across and kissed me on the mouth. My embarrassment could not undermine my pleasure.

CHAPTER SIXTEEN

And so we come to the, what some might call, 'the final straw'. Way back in this story I told you that not only was it a wild ride but in that year, when I was 17, and soon to turn 18, there were so many things going on in my life, school, Grandma, my mother, friends and enemies, Mr Moore and of course in my head that I thought if some idiot (pick an idiot, any idiot) dropped a nuclear bomb as well I wouldn't have been surprised. But I promised to tell the truth as close as I could, no matter how difficult, so I won't let up now, seeing you've come this far with me.

After my mother's funeral I went about my daily life. Me and Grandma seemed to come together, closer if that was possible. She had a small episode with her diabetes, no wonder, but this time Walter took over and I was happy for him to do it—doctor, hospital, diet—and they were beginning to look like they belonged to each other. And even though I was about to go for my licence, Grandma could probably do without another drive with me, where her nail marks were gouged into the dashboard. That really offended me but then again I presumed I was a good driver but maybe not to an old lady who wanted to get as many extra years as she could.

The film festival euphoria died away and school got back into its rhythm which I still felt was out of step with mine, and probably many others as well. I feel as though I'm showing myself to be a born again good guy who has finally dropped all his antagonism and learnt my lessons and is heading to a brilliant Year 12 the following year. Maybe there were some changes but every now and then I had to let go and allow myself some breathing space. Or some small incident would spark a sarcastic response. One of which occurred in Jack Kettle's class, which is a touch shameful considering what a good teacher he was and the way he'd have lunch with kids who could hardly read and write and turn them into literate beings, plus a number of other selfless acts. But I'm afraid nobody could be saved from my 'shit on the liver' which had been brought about by a comment made to me by some young kid who jokingly asked me, in front of his mates, when I was going to go off my head again. He was in Year 9 and didn't know that his age saved him from me. Yes some maturity was called for, after all he was just a kid showing off to his mates. Unfortunately, it didn't save Jack. The ants were off and running in my brain. Again.

By the time I got to Jack Kettle's class the ants, which had become bullants, were crawling out of my ears and other orifices, to the point where I hardly knew what I was doing or saying. Until, without thinking, I automatically fell back to my refuge of sarcasm and smart-arsedness.

Jack Kettle was well known for his personal campaign against the misuse of apostrophes. His classrooms were decked out with posters titled 'Apostrophe Man'—a superhero destined to fight the battle against the use of apostrophes every time an 's' appeared at the end of a word. Like *Fish and Chip*'s, *Video*'s, *Riverside College*'s (correct use) *student*'s (incorrect)—on and on and on. Their misuse drove Jack crazy, to the point where if you got it wrong in your class work, anything else you might have done was virtually ignored, while the apostrophe crime was dealt with in no uncertain manner. Jack had also regularly attacked the school daily bulletin on the screens around the school if the secretaries had let past an errant apostrophe or two. He was also as savage about the non-use of the apostrophe when it came to words like *you're, can't* and *don't*.

So what did I do? I slipped into my usual persona, raised my hand and asked, "Jack, I'm really confused." Confusion usually delighted him because that could lead a kid to enlightenment. He raised his eyebrows enquiringly. Roxy looked at me nervously.

"Look, I know you get really annoyed by people using apostrophes in the wrong way." The class looked up. They were used to me agreeing with Jack on this question and if the truth be told, I was about the only kid in his class to always get the dreaded apostrophe use correct.

"I thought you agreed with me, Morrison." He wandered over to his desk and sat down. Jack carried a bit of weight so when he sat we always wondered if the non-ergonomic plastic chairs could withstand the burden. "What's the problem?"

"I've been thinking about the whole thing, and I think it would be better if you gave up your apostrophe campaign."

Jack tried his best to appear calm. Getting up from his groaning seat, he said, "And why's that Morrison?" What you have to understand is that Jack was passionate about the whole thing. Saying what I did would be like me telling Grandma that she should stop barracking for the Doggies and go for another team.

"Instead of trying to get people to use them correctly, why not get rid of them altogether?!"

Jack Kettle turned visibly pale, holding the edge of his desk in case he fainted or blew up. The latter was more likely. In a soft, barely audible voice, he asked, "But how would people distinguish between *your* and *you're*? And how would we know the possessive, like *Morrison's books*, if we didn't have them. There'd be complete confusion!"

Now for the sword into the neck of the bull. The class was with me, not that that was important—it just helped the delivery. I got up and went to the whiteboard. "I think if you got rid of them completely, nobody would worry." I picked up a marker. "I'll show you what I mean. If they read something like"—I began writing on the board, *Youre an idiot. Whatre you doin stealing Jack Kettles campaign. Cant you see its wrong!*—"Everybody would understand and we could all stop worrying and stop getting annoyed every time we saw or didn't see an apostrophe."

The class laughed like crazy people and Jack, irritated by my little game, smiled like he was constipated and told the class to get on with their work. The ants scrambling in my brain had eased a bit, but poor old Jack Kettle remained flushed in the face and could barely look at me. He knew he was the butt of my sham performance, felt humiliated and showed it.

Sometimes I hated myself. Which Roxy felt was a good response to my nonsense.

"Happy now, Morrison?!" she said as she slapped me on the arm as we left the class. "Like, did that make you feel good!?" She glared at me. "What has poor bloody Jack Kettle ever done to you, mate?" I looked sheepish and couldn't hold her stare. "Really, Morrison. That was a real nasty act. I almost walked out."

She started to walk off from me, but turned and said, "Morrison, I know things, life and your life in particular hasn't been easy, especially the last few weeks, but Jack Kettle?! He's not Hamm, he's not one of the bad guys." Then Roxy walked back to me, close to my face, and she wasn't about to kiss me either. "You should go and apologise to him. If you had any balls, that's what you'd do." Then she stormed off.

The last class was Biology and I put my head down and wondered if others could see the shame emblazoned on my forehead. I can't think of too many people who can speak to me like Roxy did and if they did I could usually ignore it or think of a great comeback. Not this time.

This time I took up Frankie's offer and saw him when school finished. I told him what happened—bit like confessing my sins. Frankie smiled at Roxy's admonition and said nothing. "Haven't you got some advice Frankie? I thought you were the one I was supposed to come to?"

Frankie gathered his pad and books and stood up to leave his office. "Hang on," I said. "Is that it? You're just going to smile at me and walk off? What's going on? First Roxy and now you." I felt the lava bubbling.

Frankie looked away at something, probably the wall, and murmured, "Morrison, if you don't know what you gotta do, then all of us who think you're one of the smartest kids we know, must be wrong! See ya."

From his office window I watched as kids played footy on the oval below, down near the river. The school was quiet except for a few noisy class detentions. Finally I picked up my bag, slung it over my shoulder and went off to find Jack.

I found him in the teachers' carpark, at his car, an old Volvo that he was very proud of. He was about to get in when he saw me. He stood by his car, looking quizzically at me. Before I reached him, he asked, "What's up Morrison? Another diatribe?" Honestly, he looked so hurt I couldn't get the words out quick enough.

"Jack... apparently I've been an arsehole to you. According to Roxy and Frankie, a real arsehole. And I agree with them. No need for that stuff in class." Then the words that so many find difficult to say: "Sorry. I mean it, I'm sorry. Sometimes I feel like, y'know, and then the words just pour out, to make myself feel better. Sometimes I do feel better, but not this time..." I looked at the tyres on his car. "So sorry, Jack. I'll try and make it up to you. If you want, I'll give a test on apostrophes to the class."

Jack Kettle gave a small chuckle and got into his car. He wound down his window and said, "I don't think that'll be necessary, Morrison, but thanks for the apology." He turned on the engine and backed out. As he drove away he suddenly stopped and beckoned me to his car. "Yes, you were a bit nasty Morrison, but I'll tell you something between you and me—that stuff you said about apostrophes—you might have a point. Maybe Apostrophe Man has a new challenge—get rid of them completely." He smiled broadly, "Then again, maybe not."

Of course my 'apostrophe' performance wasn't the final straw. I suspect I was acting badly because I hadn't seen old Mr Moore around. Not that it happened much these days, but

I hadn't had the pleasure of sitting in Morrison's chair nor any reason to hang out at the front office. I told this to Roxy who had rewarded my apology with hugs and kisses and was talking to me again since my mea culpa to Jack Kettle.

"No, I haven't seen him at all," said Roxy. "Why don't you go around to his house. Maybe there's something up with Jenny." In all the hubbub of recent times I hadn't thought about the trials and tribulations of the old guy. I knew I wouldn't concentrate on anything school had to offer me in the afternoon, so I feigned sickness to Frankie who knew it was a lie in metre-high letters, but cut me some slack, most likely due to my act of contrition.

"D'you think you'll be back tomorrow?" he asked, a smile at the corners of his mouth. "And what about Roxy? She sick as well?"

"No, just me. She's very healthy as far as I know."

I almost ran out of school. No bus was in sight, so I jogged to Mr Moore's house. I hate jogging almost as much as I hate the bush, but my sudden awareness of Mr Moore's absence had got the alarm bells ringing. The house looked empty. Some wattle birds were squabbling in the low bushes that grew under the front windows. I rang the bell which echoed down the hallway, into the lounge room and out to the kitchen. I knew the bell was the same bell it had always been, but its ringing sounded lost and forlorn. I went around the side of the house to a side gate which was unlocked. I started to call out, "Mr Moore, Mr Moore" as I peered inside windows and finally found myself out the back where I rattled and banged on the door. Unless Mr Moore and his wife were inside hiding from that strange boy, Morrison, nobody was home. It felt like there'd been nobody there for days.

I went back along the side path and was opening the front gate when a car pulled up. The driver got out, a frown on her face until she realised it was me. "Morrison. What're you doing here?" asked Grace, Jenny's carer. "Shouldn't you be at school?" she said, checking her watch.

"No, all cool Grace. Gave me the afternoon off. New system they got."

Grace smiled, not believing a word. She met me at the gate. "I suppose you've come to see Mr Moore. Things are a bit bad at the moment, Morrison. Jenny, Mrs Moore's been in hospital for a week now. She has pneumonia but now they've discovered a clot in her lung."

I gripped the gate. "But she's only got Alzheimer's hasn't she? I know it gets worse but pneumonia, clots, what's going on?"

Grace held my arm. "I know, I know. But they have less and less resistance to infections. Not looking too good. Mr Moore is with her all the time. He's been sleeping on a foam mattress next to her bed."

The sight of him sleeping next to his wife, probably as she lay dying, was too strong an image and my eyes filled to the brim. Grace put her arms around me in a now sad little street in Ballantyne and held me close. And I let her. After a while I asked if I could go into the hospital, but she advised me not to. "I think all Bill wants is to sit with her. I don't think she's got long. I was coming back for a few things he needed."

It was late afternoon by the time I arrived at Buckland's Jetty. I called Grandma to tell her about Mr Moore and Jenny and that I wouldn't be home till late. I didn't call Roxy. I didn't try and visit Mrs Moore. I went to where I was pretty sure my soul lived, where my spirit resided. I got there at five, sat on the end of the pier and stayed for I don't know how long. My Māori fisherman turned up at nine and sometime later, put down his rod and walked over to me. He squatted next to me and didn't say a word. He remained like that for some time and then, with a huge hand placed on my shoulder, he said, "It'll get better, mate. It usually does." And returned to his fishing.

Mrs Moore died two days later, due to 'complications'. And that was 'the final straw' I was talking about. You see, if all the mess from the last year hadn't happened, then Mrs

Moore's death would've been just that—a death that had little impact on me. But now—now—this was different. This was bloody awful. Mr Moore, my friend, a man who I trusted, who somehow kept an eye out for me—Jenny, his wife had died.

I told Grandma, Roxy, little Terry, Petticoat Boy, Frankie, Jack Kettle, Ms Rosario, Stan and Izzie, Ms Gerrard... . It was so out of character for me to do something like this, but I wanted to be the one to tell the news. I wanted to let my part of the world know that a calamity had taken place. Church and Town Hall bells should have been pealing. News bulletins should have led with this story of Mrs Moore's death. But she wasn't a politician, a rock star, a member of the Royal family, an entrepreneur, cashed-up businesswoman. Jenny Moore was the lifelong mate of Bill Moore, and even though I hardly knew her, if she loved the old Mr Moore for as long as she did, she must've been lovely.

Apart from telling friends of her death, I wanted to do something for Mr Moore. I had no idea what to do. I didn't discuss this with anybody. Sure I could go to the funeral, take flowers, take one of Grandma's casseroles around to him (although, as I've told you, she wasn't the best cook around), write him a special card—it all seemed so predictable, so ordinary, so unlike what Mr Moore meant to me. For days I plagued myself with this question. The third day after her death I took the bus to Mr Moore's house. As I approached there were piles of cars parked along the street. I stood at the gate and felt like an outsider, so I hurriedly left before someone who recognised me emerged and felt as though they had to invite me in. I left a card in his letterbox which Grandma had bought for me. For a person who loves writing, the best I could dredge up was: "Dear Mr Moore. I am so sorry. Morrison."

The funeral came round. It was a Thursday and the school had determined that as long as you had a note from home, students could attend. If I'd been Mr Moore it would've been the last thing I wanted—all the grubby students going to his wife's funeral. Seeing him in his pain and despair. But what am I talking about? I was going to be one of them. It was held in an old Uniting Church, red bricks, leadlight windows, vaulted ceilings with religious paintings on the walls. Up the front was a high pulpit and to the side was a small, modern organ. Flowers were everywhere, mainly white and cream lilies in ceramic and brass vases. A large bible lay open on a lectern.

I went with Grandma and Walter, who let me drive to the church. It was only a few days till I turned eighteen and Walter had offered to take me to my test. I met Roxy and the other two misfits outside and we went straight inside because there were so many mourners. All the usual suspects were there, teachers—some who I approved of and others, well... . Maybe twenty students, and down the front was a man who looked like an older version of Mr Moore and next to him was a woman about my mother's age—which set off comparisons and memories of that other funeral. As the church began to bulge with the swelling numbers, I watched the dark mahogany coffin and fervently prayed that there'd be no repeat performance of lids being swung open and dead people, like Jenny, sitting up having a chat—perhaps playing with one of her snowdomes. We sat halfway up the rows of pews, with me on the aisle. As soon as the service started I went into some kind of a reverie. It wasn't that I didn't care what was said or the memories that were shared, it was for two reasons. First, after everything that had happened, I didn't think I could cope with yet another sad event. "Too much, too much," my brain yelled. But the second reason, and the most important, was that I hadn't been able to come up with anything that would take away some of Mr Moore's pain, nothing that would give him something to hang onto. Something I could give him, something I could do for him. No idea came close. For the whole service that was all that occupied my mind. So it was a surprise when it ended and they carried the coffin out, followed by Mr Moore, relatives and friends. And it was a surprise when Mr Moore recognised me through his tears, stopped and affectionately shook hands with me. His brother and daughter smiled at me, with no clue who this kid was, then guided the old guy along the blue carpeted aisle, outside to the waiting hearse.

I leant over to Roxy and whispered, "Thought of something."

MORRISON & MR MOORE

The Buffalo River finds its way down from high autumn plains and mountains, snaking its way through farmlands, old tobacco fields and smoking mills. Wide in stretches, framed by grey boulders and pebbled beaches. Sometimes shallow, running over sandy stretches where fish twist and jump heading upstream. It gathers in dark blue pools, bordered by native pines and lemon scented gums and then, from this tranquillity finds itself tumbling through a puzzle of unyielding rocks.

Past one of these rapids the river slows and meanders by a small camp site, where two men, one young and one elderly, have set up camp. The old man tends to a campfire circled by river rocks. He returns to the younger one who inexpertly holds onto a fishing line that lies in wait in the water. Next to them, glinting in the late afternoon sun, three pan-sized trout lie on a flat rock. The line goes taut, then jags and without any words, the young guy quickly hands the rod to the old bloke. With a swift jerk, he reels in yet another rainbow trout.

Later that night, with full bellies, they drink and talk around the fire, but mostly they don't talk. The moon has been full but now the bush and the river darken as clouds blanket the dome of stars. A currawong gives a last call—'good night, sleep tight.'

The old man gets up from the log he is seated on, and poking the fire, he says, "How did you think of this, son?"

The young man twirls a burning stick in the red coals. "Wasn't hard. Only had to look at the interview again. It was obvious then."

The other smiled. "Really? I must look at it again, myself." Sighing, he says, "Have to get back tomorrow. My brother wants me to move up there with him. Cairns. But I don't know. What about you?"

"Well, sir. Don't think I'll do Year 12. You probably think that's a bad move."

The old man shrugged.

"Think I'll do a writing course somewhere. See how that goes."

"And what do you think you'll write. Crime? Romance? Adventure?"

"Not sure. But I've got an idea. John Morrison reckons that if a writer didn't have a certain experience he wouldn't have written the story. It's what he does with truth that makes the story."

In a shadowed tree a mopoke agreed. The river babbled and the night stretched, yawned and went on its way.

About the Author

Michael Hyde taught in working class secondary schools for 25 years, where he established successful writing cultures across a number of schools. He lectured in tertiary institutions, mainly at Victoria University, for 20 years where he taught and co-ordinated Creative Writing, Sports Writing and Children's Literature. He was awarded the Vice-Chancellors award for Teaching Excellence. He gained his PhD for the thesis 'The Sixties—the lived experience' which also produced his memoir, *All Along the Watchtower*—one of the very few accounts of that period.

Michael has been writing since the mid 1970's and since then he has published thirty-six books, both fiction and non-fiction. He writes for children (*Girls Change the Game*) but is mainly known for his Young Adult novels, especially MAX, *Tyger Tyger*, *Hey Joe*, *Surfing Goliath*, and *Footy Dreaming*.

He has four children and two grandchildren, and lives in the bush with his wife, Gabrielle. He loves writing (of course), the sea, rivers, canoeing, playing hand drums, veggie gardening, beach walking, music, cooking, and is an avid reader. He also loves sport, footy and is a Collingwood tragic.

To contact Michael, his website is:

michaelhyde.com.au